El Cazador

(The Hunter)

El Cazador

(The Hunter)

A Novel   R. M. Lienau

SUNSTONE
PRESS

SANTA FE

Sunstone books may be purchased for educational, business, or sales promotional use.
For information please write: Special Markets Department, Sunstone Press,
P.O. Box 2321, Santa Fe, New Mexico 87504-2321.
Cover art by Jime Wimmer
Book and Cover design by Vicki Ahl
Body typeface › Adobe Jenson Pro
Printed on acid-free paper
∞
eBook 978-1-61139-513-6

Library of Congress Cataloging-in-Publication Data

Names: Lienau, R. M. (Richard M.), author.
Title: El cazador (the hunter) : a novel / by R.M. Lienau.
Description: Santa Fe : Sunstone Press, 2017.
Identifiers: LCCN 2017026635 (print) | LCCN 2017029785 (ebook) | ISBN
9781611395136 | ISBN 9781632931788 (softcover : alk. paper)
Subjects: LCSH: Revenge--Fiction. | GSAFD: Adventure fiction.
Classification: LCC PS3562.I4533 (ebook) | LCC PS3562.I4533 C37 2017 (print)
| DDC 813/.54--dc23
LC record available at https://lccn.loc.gov/2017026635

SUNSTONE PRESS IS COMMITTED TO MINIMIZING OUR ENVIRONMENTAL IMPACT ON THE PLANET. THE PAPER USED IN THIS BOOK IS FROM
RESPONSIBLY MANAGED FORESTS. OUR PRINTER HAS RECEIVED CHAIN OF CUSTODY (COC) CERTIFICATION FROM: THE FOREST STEWARDSHIP
COUNCIL™ (FSC®), PROGRAMME FOR THE ENDORSEMENT OF FOREST CERTIFICATION™ (PEFC™), AND THE SUSTAINABLE FORESTRY INITIATIVE® (SFI®).
THE FSC® COUNCIL IS A NON-PROFIT ORGANIZATION, PROMOTING THE ENVIRONMENTALLY APPROPRIATE, SOCIALLY BENEFICIAL AND
ECONOMICALLY VIABLE MANAGEMENT OF THE WORLD'S FORESTS. FSC® CERTIFICATION IS RECOGNIZED INTERNATIONALLY AS A
RIGOROUS ENVIRONMENTAL AND SOCIAL STANDARD FOR RESPONSIBLE FOREST MANAGEMENT.

WWW.SUNSTONEPRESS.COM
SUNSTONE PRESS / POST OFFICE BOX 2321 / SANTA FE, NM 87504-2321 /USA
(505) 988-4418 / ORDERS ONLY (800) 243-5644 / FAX (505) 988-1025

Acknowledgment and Dedication

This story owes its origin to a very likable and talented man; the stage, screen and television actor, Victor Joseph Izay.

Many years ago, when he and I lived in the Los Angeles, California area, he showed me a poem he had written. It was about a *Penitente* village in northern New Mexico, the state where we had met years earlier in our mutual involvement with legitimate theater. The *"Penitentes,"* or Penitents, at least in New Mexico, are an offshoot of the Catholic religion, in which the members, all men, practice mutual- and auto-flagellation, as well as faux crucifixion, usually during the Easter season. The rise of this ardent religious organization in New Mexico, traceable to ancient Greek culture, was caused in the main by the fact that the central core of the Catholic Church and its clergy had abandoned New Mexico due to political upheaval in Mexico, which had ruled the region until that period. Thus the *Penitentes* stood in for the clergy in their own, "unofficial," special way. Although there are fewer today, during one period, they were strong in what is now that state, more so in outlying villages than in the population centers.

His poem was the brief tale of one such village, an outrage committed against it, and the hero who avenged it through his singular efforts.

I suggested to him that we collaborate on a screenplay based upon it, and he agreed. Shortly into our mutual effort, his sweet wife, Connie, died of a devastating illness. Inconsolable, he felt he could go no further with the writing effort. After some time, I asked him if he would allow me to continue alone, and he agreed. I assured him I would submit to him whatever I wrote for his approval. A few months later, with his blessing, I finished the script.

Those who are aware of the script, especially those who have read it, have encouraged me to write the story in novel form; thus the following.

It is to his fond memory and that of Connie, and to his fine children, Victoria, Greg and Steve, that I dedicate this work.

—R. M. Lienau
Pecos, New Mexico
July, 2016

1

The pitch-black, not yet moon-bright night sky above the mountain village of San Blas, in the Territory of New Mexico, was pocked with a dome of brilliant, twinkling stars. It was chilly, despite the time of year, April, in what was then shortly after the Mexican War.

Although the middle of the night, well past the hour when most of the villagers, especially children, were snug in their poor beds, they gathered in the plaza at random as they trickled in from all directions through the crazy-quilt pattern of paths between predominantly low, flat-roofed adobe houses. They formed, as they had on many occasions, into a column of ranks three and four abreast. They shuffled slowly toward the village church on the northern verge of the square, with its twin steeples between which was a crooked wooden cross. Most held lighted candles reverently against the chill dark. The orange flames, protected against flame-out with their cupped hands, flickered and danced, moved by a light breeze that wove intermittently through the village.

They were dressed for the cold night and the special event in their best, which was also poor. The women wore long dresses, mostly black, as were their lace-fringed shawls, or *rebosos*, draped over their heads and shoulders and down their backs. Most of the men wore loose, white *pantalones*, tied at the ankles. Some, those who could afford them, had *ponchos* draped over their bodies; others covered themselves with simple blankets. A few wore soled, lace-up shoes on their labor-worn feet; many others scuffed along in sandals. Some wore soft deer skin moccasins purchased with trade at a near-by Native American Pueblo. A few, as an expression of religious fervor, were barefoot. The children, boys and girls alike, as young as five, straggle-marched with the adults, and were outfitted in similar fashion. Among them was a man who piped a *pito*, attendant with an *alabado*, a religious chant, mumbled here and there in the reverent gathering.

While most of the people moved toward the open doors of the old adobe church, several of the men, most of whom wore black jackets, separated to join another group of men who had formed up earlier and moved in another direction. These were men of the *Penitente* order. They were headed for the *Morada*, their secret and sacred meeting house. With them was the *pito* player, who continued his woeful piping.

Meanwhile, the majority of the celebrants, for the most part women, children and older men, entered the church. Its soft, crude earthen walls and open-beam ceiling, with its gaudily painted wainscot, glowed in a golden hue engendered by eerie, flickering light that emanated from dozens of candles ensconced in hand-made candelabra along the walls and in the colorfully-decorated nave. Few were able to sit, since there lacked a sufficient number of locally-made benches. Those who stood, mostly the youngest and ablest among them, huddled behind the *bancos* all the way to the front of the building, near the opening onto the plaza. Those who were able to sit, were the aged or infirm. Some dropped to their knees and raised their hands in a gesture of reverence and prayer on the smooth, bare dirt floor.

The different songs some sang during the march, now coalesced into a single a capella hymn. This was lead, not by a priest, since the village had none, but by a middle-aged man, a village-appointed deacon, who stood in front of the simple, but gaudy altar with an old hymnal open in his outstretched hands.

The men who diverted from the main crowd in the *plaza* moved along a path that led up an incline beyond the church and houses that clustered around the square and its dominant house of worship. They fell in with a group of men, now some twenty-strong, who moved slowly at a shuffling gate. They were slow because of three men at the front of the procession who were being tortured as they moved along shoulder to shoulder. The two outside men were barefoot and nearly as naked as was the man at their center. His head, unlike theirs, was ringed with thorns. All three wore knives that dangled from their thighs that caused bloody cuts on their ankles.

The thorn-crowned man was Polito Torres. He had been selected by the elders of the society, and with the acquiescence of the village, to play the part of the *Cristo* in the *Penitente* passion play. The other two men, without the crown of thorns, played the parts of the criminals who were to be crucified along with the central character of the Christ, Jesus.

Immediately ahead of the three suffering men, who were close to freezing in the cold mountain air, was the *Hermano Mayor*, the Senior Brother, leader of the secret religious society, who lead the way. He, as did the church deacon, read the words of the chanted *alabado* from a small secret book. Alongside him was the *pito* player, as he piped a dissonant tune to the rambling religious chant. Behind the three men destined for crucifixion came the beaters. They, in turn, carried whips, chains and cactus-bearing rods with which they struck the faux condemned as they struggled along. This action added to the painful, bloody wounds on the backs and legs of the central players. Some of the men in the following group carried chains and other auto-flagellation devices with which they beat themselves as they moved and chanted. All but the *Hermano Mayor* were without footwear.

Soon the column came to a small, two-room adobe building. Set in front of the single low door was a crude, six-foot high wooden cross that rested at an angle in a pyramid of stones. A name was carved into the staff; "*Calvario*," or Calvary. A man stood next to the door with a crude, hand-made wooden *matraca*, which made a staccato rattling sound as he swung it.

As the chant continued with the playing of the flute, the *Hermano* entered, followed single-file by members of the brotherhood, some of whom who had to duck as they passed beneath the low wooden lintel of the narrow opening. A few men, non-members who had followed, disbursed, while an even smaller group remained at a respectful distance to hold vigil through the night as they moved about, blew their breaths against their cold hands and stomped their feet in an attempt to stay warm. Near the door were two of the black-jacketed brothers who stood guard, there to prevent any outsiders from entering the sacred building, a highly unlikely occurrence.

In the center of the first room was a heavy table of thick local pine around which stood members of the brotherhood as they continued the chant to the accompaniment of the *pito*, the rattling *matraca* and the reading by the *Hermano Mayor*. Opposite the open door to the outside was a small altar. Close to the ceiling in one outer wall were two gun-slit windows, parallel to the floor. To one side of the centered altar was another door which lead into an inner room. Two of the brothers carried tall, thin wooden crosses which reached to within a few inches of the ceiling with its narrow beams of hand de-barked pine. The room would have been dark save for lighted tapers in wall-mounted sconces and others on the table.

The chant died down as the *Hermano Mayor* ceased the recital, turned and moved slowly for the inner door and then into the room beyond. The others filed in behind him until all were in the windowless room. The leader, his book still in hand, stood near a corner fireplace alight with *piñon* and cedar logs. Its flames were the only source of long-shadow casting, flickering, dancing, yellow-orange light. He waited until most of the brothers were seated on the dirt floor, while the remainder stood. In the corner opposite the fireplace stood a man who rattled a chain menacingly as the *Hermano Mayor* began to recite a ritual tale, this also read from the sacred book. Next to him was the *Cristo*, dressed in nothing more than a loin cloth, while the two faux criminals stood as part of the audience.

He shivered from the cold, pain and exhaustion. His hands were bound with horsehair, and rivulets of blood coursed down from his head and neck. A crown of thorns remained around his head. Two beaters hit him rhythmically with leather thongs as the tale rose in timbre and intensity.

After a long night, and the fire had died to embers and the room became dark, the men rose and followed the *Hermano Mayor*, the beaters and the *Cristo*, who had collapsed onto the bare earthen floor, and was dragged into the front room. There, four men lifted a four-foot tall, stark and frightening plaster image of the Christ on a pole litter. It was crowned with thorns and blood in the classical representation.

Grey, pre-dawn light bathed the village as the men of the *Penitente* order exited the *Morada*. First came the men bearing the Christ litter, followed by the *Hermano Mayor*, the *pito* player and the *matraca* swinger. Behind them, barely able to walk, was the beaten, bloody and pain-wracked *Cristo*. Behind him were his tormentors, the beaters, and the remainder of the troop, all who chanted. The *Cristo* was provided a large, heavy wooden cross, which he barely managed to shoulder as the beaters continued to whip him.

The other men to be crucified followed with their tormentors. They were now hobbled with horsehair ropes, and their hands were tied. They were, as was the *Cristo*, fitted with cacti around their waists.

Accompanying all were auto-flagellants, who punished themselves with whips and cactus. They were also without footwear.

Beyond and above them rose the sacred hill called *Calvario*, or Calvary. It was in stark relief against the brightening morning sky above the line of mountain ridges and peaks to the east. There, two crosses stood apart with a space between for a third.

Since the youngest of the children had been relegated to their beds, it was then that those who braved the night in the church, primarily adults, began to file out into the brisk morning. They were tired, hungry and thirsty, but their passion carried them. Four women, covered in black from head to toe, appeared bearing a litter similar to that borne by the *Penitentes*. It was the *Madre dolorosa*, or "sad mother," a depiction of Mary, the mother of Christ. Unlike her son carried on the other litter, she was dressed in colorful, decorative clothing, lovingly made by the women of the village. There was something starkly frightful in her sad, staring, unsmiling visage, which compounded the emotions of the moment.

Other villagers, adults and youths alike, those who had not braved the long, half-lit vigil in the earthen church, straggled into the plaza and joined the coalescing procession. As they hurried to join the *Penitente* march, most mumbled prayers and crossed themselves repeatedly. Some were barefoot against the cold, hard ground.

Both processions merged as they moved slowly up the slope to *Calvario*. The rising timbre of the chant, accompanied by the high-pitched piping of the *pito* and the rattle of the *matraca* were joined by agitated, barking dogs. Along with the sounds from the crowd and the attendant animals, the crowing of cocks added to the cacophony. The first bright rays of warming sunlight streamed over the crest of the mountain. It began to warm the bodies of the reverent villagers and the high, thin air.

Along the march, the two litters bearing the likenesses of the holy family were brought together, side-by-side. The litter bearers tilted the figures toward each other such that they appeared to be speaking; the *Madre* whispering a grieving, final farewell to her doomed son; her son barely able to comprehend. In response, the chant rose in volume along with "Oohs" and "Aahs" emitted by the faithful. Some dropped to their knees, their palms offered to the sky, and wept at the sight. The Penitente brothers remained stoical and continued on their mission, unaffected by the scene played out around them.

At the head of the procession of brothers and villagers, was the cross-bearing Polito as the *Cristo*, flanked by the two criminals. Ahead of the three desperate actors was the *Hermano Mayor*, the *pito* player and the *matraca* wielder. Behind both were the beaters, who continued to torment the three doomed men. As a part of the passion play, some of the participants shouted comments, both sympathetic and damning, at the men about to be crucified.

One of the villagers, a young woman, as were most of the other women, shrouded in a black lace *reboso*, walked closely behind the beaters. Her name was Nicanora, the wife of Polito, who played the grueling part of the *Cristo* in the realistic *Penitente* play. Her face, wet with tears, was wracked with a combination of sympathy, sorrow and pride as she watched her husband's halting, painful struggle up the incline to the spot where the center cross was to be placed. Others, mainly women, shared her response to the extraordinary spectacle.

Above the scene being played out by the villagers of San Blas, the mountains were covered here and there with traces of late snow and a mantle of clouds which caused the cold early morning light to come and go, which served to further dramatize the ancient ritual. Brief zephyrs careened through the town of squat, brown houses as the light came and went. Dust rose here and there along the paths between the houses, along the worn path and up to the hill called *Calvario*.

2

S anto, who stood straight, but no taller than his ability to see over a
saddled horse, was outside his humble house on the western outskirt
of the small town. In his late eighties, he was balding, with a fringe of
greying hair above his ears. Healthy from trekking into the nearby *floresta*
for wood, then chopping and splitting it for his fireplace and cookstove, his
bright hazel eyes and almost line-free face betrayed a kind, happy, friendly
old man. Against the brisk morning air, he wore a colorful woolen jacket
crafted by his long-deceased wife, mother of his four grown, but absent,
children.

He looked from his vantage point toward the distant activities on
the hill beyond the eastern verge of the village, then turned as he heard the
familiar sounds made by the hooves of a horse moving at a walking pace.

The man on the great black horse was in his mid-twenties. Erect
in the saddle, he wore a leather vest over a flowered cotton shirt. On his
head was a broad-brimmed, black, military-style hat with oak tassels. The
britches over his black leather military boots were a light tan. On his right,
a single-shot Sharps carbine was nestled in a Cheyenne-made leather
scabbard decorated with leather fringes along its length. A Dakota warrior
symbol was carved into the thick bison hide close to the shoulder piece of
the long gun. A fringed and beaded sheath held a deer horn- handled hunting knife against his likewise beaded leather belt. Behind his saddle was a
tan bedroll, and on either side were swollen leather saddlebags. Along with
a skin canteen that drooped from the pommel, was a leather quirt coiled
about it. Although young, his countenance was that of a man of friendly,
knowing wisdom; one who had seen and borne conflict. Handsome to all
who knew him, man and woman alike, he comported himself as self-confi-
dent and -reliant.

Santo looked up with a broad grin as the horse drew near. "Severino! Severino, is that you?!" He took a step forward as he squinted up at the rider.

As his mount wheezed to a reluctant halt with vapor emitting from his large nostrils into the cold morning air, Severino touched the brim of his hat and leaned forward to rest his arm on the pommel ridge. "It is I." He looked around, then down at the old man. "How goes it, Santo? Where is everyone? The streets are empty."

"Severino! It has been such a long time! Two years! Has it been two years?" He advanced closer as he rubbed his chin and his mouth.

"More. That and six months." He paused, then jerked his chin upward and looked toward the town. "Where are the others?" He peered down at Santo.

"It is Easter. They are on the hill." He looked away, then up as he licked his lips. "They say you were with the gringos in their army."

"Of course. Easter." He sat up, sobered, adjusted his hat, then spoke. "No. I killed buffalo for them. For meat. And tracked. Who is the Cristo?"

Santo took two paces away, looked down, then up. "I helped to watch over your house and your orchard. Uh—the young vines—they are doing well." He paused to frame his next statement. "I chased off some poachers, but—"

Severino removed his hat, returned it to his head, adjusted it, looked again toward *Calvario*, then down at Santo. "I am much obliged, Santo. Who is the Cristo?" A cut had come to his voice.

Santo looked away, then moved his head back and forth to avoid Severino's glare. "Did you fight for them? We heard you did some fighting."

Severino smiled wryly, closed his eyes, then opened them as his patience waned. He dropped his voice. "I had my share."

"Against the Indians?"

"With some and against some." He looked away, his mouth firm.

Santo went quiet, looked down, then up at the returnee. "There will be those who will not be happy to see you return. Perhaps you should have waited." His voice rose in timbre as he wrinkled his brow and held his arms out wide, palms up. He shook his head.

Severino glared down at him. "Why?! This is my home! Let those unhappy with me leave!" He waved his arm in a wide arc. "Now I ask you again! Who is the Cristo?!"

Santo shook his head, looked down, then up. "Ay, God, Severino. Your brother, Polito." He rubbed his hands together in frustration.

Severino sat up straight, arched his back, and stared intently toward *Calvario* as his features darkened and his mind went elsewhere. Then he clicked his horse forward.

With his voice raised, Santo spoke to Severino's back. "We told him he should not. He has had a bad time, he and Nicanora. It was so sad." His voice trailed off, then he continued, almost to himself as Severino was out of earshot. "Nicanora almost died with the baby, but the baby died instead." He shouted, "We told him—" Then he shook his old head and gestured with his hands as he stared at the ground.

Severino was unable to hear him. If he had been close, he would not have heard him anyway.

Santo, the smile gone, turned and moved slowly into his house and shut the door gently.

As Severino rode slowly along the main road into the village, he kept his eyes on the activity on the hill when it became visible past and over the tops of the low dwellings. Here and there, some of the villagers who remained away from the religious ceremony watched as he moved past. Some recognized him and began a house-to-house whispering campaign. No one spoke to him, and if he had bothered to look, no one waved, while a very few smiled, and many frowned at his passing. Several noisy little boys ran alongside accompanied by a pair of yapping dogs. Despite the lack of positive greeting, he doffed his hat more than once to a woman who appeared in her doorway and looked at him.

Past the plaza and the little church, he made his way up the slope opposite to that which lead to *Calvario*. Ahead lay his small property with the house, animal pens, orchard and fallow field he alone had established.

As he came close to the buildings, and after he had made a cursory inspection, he reigned his horse around so he could see the ceremony across the small intervening valley. He saw that three crosses had been raised, and made out the crowd that faced them. He heard enough of the sounds from the other hill to know that they resulted from the chanting of the *alabado* along with the crude, locally-made instruments that accompanied the a capella singing.

He patted his horses neck, dismounted, then lead him to the corral and lean-to shelter provided for the animal. After he had removed and stowed the saddle and leathers, he ensured that the horse had feed and snow-melt water. From there, he entered his unlocked house and walked into the cold, dark, dusty front room.

He had built the small two-room house of adobes he had made from the soil that surrounded the house, mixed with some of the clean bottom silt from a nearby stream along with straw from his own field. The ceiling was of cedar *latias* supported by pine *vigas* cut from the wood-giving *floresta* that rose into the high mountain terrain beyond the village. The roof, as were those of the village, an extension of the ceiling, was of eight inches of local clay, set at a mild angle to ensure runoff from rain and snow. The doors, door and window frames, he had cut from pine logs and hand-adzed to shape. The glass for the three windows were purchased at the only town store.

He laid his saddlebags and bedroll on the floor near the entrance, leaned the Sharps against the wall, and went to the pot-bellied wood stove that sat in a corner. He opened the cast iron door, then placed three pieces of firewood onto the fire grate over some kindling. With a match from his vest pocket, he started the flame which rose quickly against the well-cured pine wood.

He watched the fire for a few seconds, then turned and walked out onto the porch that graced the front of the house. He peered closely at the scene on the opposite hill as he tried to discern the activity. Strains of the voices, the *pito* and the *matraca* drifted in and out as his eyes began to wet. He was six when he first heard those sounds. They meant little to him at first. Later, they would mean everything.

The little boy was almost smothered by the crowd around him. He looked up at the man bound to the cross. He was the boy's father, and even the boy realized that his father suffered. He watched as he shook violently as the cuts and bruises on his thin, frail body oozed dark, red blood that ran down his face, neck, chest, belly, over the thin loin cloth and onto his twitching legs, then to his white, almost bloodless feet. He saw his father's lips as they seemed to cry out to those who watched below. The boy was frightened by the sounds that crowded in on him. The uncoordinated chanting, the pitero *with his wailing flute, the* matraca-*bearer, the moaning and crying . . . He saw his father's head flop to one side as the shaking and moaning ceased. Then the crowd went silent, the* pito *made one last woeful sound, and the wooden* matraca *went silent. The three women at the base of the cross, which included his mother, on their knees, stopped their prayers as they reacted to the sudden change about them. They looked up to see. The boy, knowing what it meant, wrested loose from his mother's grip, pushed through the mass of confused people and ran as fast as he could.*

Behind him, at first he heard the cry, then as he ran, it became faint, as his brother, Polito, four years his senior, called after him. "Severino! Severino! Hey! Come back! You must not run away! Come back!" Then Polito chased after him.

As he clutched his mother's skirt, the boy looked down into the deep grave. He watched as a lizard poised, then scurried across the simple wooden, sun-drenched coffin with a pot-metal cross nailed to the head end. Then he saw and heard the dry, brown dirt as it was thrown onto the coffin. It was loud; too loud. He clung to his mother as the dirt piled higher. He looked up at the priest. He saw his petulant wet mouth move, but he was unable to hear the words the old, porcine man uttered. He looked up at his weeping mother. He knew she was crying, because he saw the way her tears pasted the dark lace veil over her face to her wet cheeks.

He looked past his mother to his brother, Polito, who stood sto-ically on her other side. His hands hung loose at his side, unmoving. It was then that he looked down once more at the crude wooden body holder and burst into tears. He reacted to his torment and grief by brushing away the saline water in a bitter, defiant gesture of hate and frustration.

The sun was eight o'clock high and warming as he broke from his reverie, turned, entered the house and closed the door. The fire in the little cast-iron pot belly stove was ablaze. He went to it, stood and warmed his hands against the chill of the room.

3

There were six of them.

In the lead was Clyde Hobson. He was not tall, but a little more than average height for the time; standing five feet and ten inches. With a ruddy, light-skinned face in need of a shave, he was lithe, with strong arm and leg muscles gained from outdoor work for most of his twenty-nine years. Though the sun was up and warmed the morning, he wore a fleece-lined jacket. On his head was a broad-brimmed felt hat, grey in color. In need of trimming and training, his dark brown hair flowed from under it, over his ears and down the back of his neck. His unadorned brown boots were scuffed and in need of new soles. Beneath the jacket, he wore a plain tan shirt and blue denim pants. Coiled at an angle around his saddle pommel was a long leather whip. His eyes and the set of his mouth had a sullen, suspicious cast.

The other five were Whitey, T.J. Cory, Bert Antrim, the eldest, then Chet and Barney. To a man they had the look of hungry drifters whose clothes and hats had seen better days. All were armed with .44 or .36 caliber Colt's revolvers holstered at their sides. All of their horses and saddles were in decent condition. All carried saddlebags and bedrolls for nights in the open. None had a long gun; a rifle or carbine.

Barney, the youngest of them at nineteen, was also the tallest, at nearly six feet. He had long red hair, and had yet to require a daily shave.

As the men on horseback rode below the rise at the west end of San Blas then came within sight of the village, Clyde pulled on the reins and slowed his pace. The others, save for T.J., followed suit. They were "gringos," a term developed during the recent war in Mexico and they were on the outskirts of a town where only the rare individual spoke a few words in English. But they were hungry and thirsty, and they had firearms in a place where only the occasional individual possessed one.

Clyde raised his hand to the brim of his hat to shade his eyes against the low morning sun.

"Whtta' ya think, Clyde?" T.J. asked.

"About what?" Clyde replied without turning his head. There was disapproval in his voice. Clyde barely tolerated his trail partner.

"Why, the town, of course."

"Jee-zuz, T.J., what in blue blazes am I to think of this here place?! This is my first time, fer Chrissakes!" He threw T.J. a sidelong glance, then returned to the study of his surroundings.

"Mess-kins, I reckon," T.J. muttered under his breath.

Bert brought his horse alongside Clyde. He spoke without looking at the man to his side. "Kinda' odd. Nobody around. These folks are almost always up and busy at daybreak. Kinda' odd."

Whitey's horse pranced a step as he spoke. "Lookie yonder, an' yew can see some milling about. Past the houses there." He pointed.

Chet clicked his horse forward until he was abreast of Clyde's other side. "Yeah. Fer sure somethin'."

Clyde clicked his tongue twice, tugged the reins, and his horse moved forward. "Well, hot damn. Don't make me no never mind. I gotta' wet my whistle and put somethin' in my belly, by damn."

"Need to find us an eatery," T.J. said.

"God, T.J., if you ain't the prophetic one," Clyde sneered, then smirked privately at his own words as his entire body reacted to the horse's movements.

"Well—" T.J. uttered. He waggled his head and re-arranged his hat.

All the others but Barney, lost in his private thoughts, laughed.

The horses did not need instruction to follow Clyde's mount.

As the pack moved slowly and cautiously into the village past the first houses, they were greeted by two dogs that circled and barked. A middle-aged woman opened her door to see what the commotion was about, took a brief look at the intruders and retreated. Santo also came to his door, curious at the commotion. Both of the villagers knew instantly who these men were and what they might represent. Santo remained in his doorway and watched. The genuine smile he had for Severino had long disappeared.

A door two houses away from that belonging to Santo opened, and a child of three ran happily into the dirt street. He was followed by a girl of sixteen, Gloria, who called out to the errant boy. The child stopped and looked her way with childish glee as she spied the six men who rode past. Her eyes went wide and her mouth dropped open, then she scooped up the laughing baby and ran back to the house. There, she put the child down and looked toward the gringos. Chet spotted her, fell back and pulled his mount to a stop, where he stared at the teenaged girl. Gloria looked at him, made brief, fearful eye contact, then disappeared inside and slammed the door shut.

Chet jerked the reins, which caused his horse to step backwards. "Shee-ut! Boy, howdy!" he exclaimed.

Bert, who noticed the brief transaction between Chet and the girl, pulled his horse close to Chet's. "Back off, Chet. That ain't fer you."

Chet looked at Bert with a frown. "What?! A man kin wonder and think about it, cain't he?"

"Yeah, I suppose, but this ain't the place to do somethin' about it." He lowered his head to look at Chet from under his eyebrows.

"Hell's fire, Bert." With his reply, which carried a trace of lilting adolescent guilt, Chet urged his horse on. He swung his head back and forth in frustration.

The rest of the crew had reined their horses to a stop as Clyde peered intently toward the other end of the town. He looked toward Bert, then Whitey. He tilted his head to one side. "Hey, Whitey, what's goin' on up yonder. Crosses an' like that." He pointed.

Whitey, who had spent time in Mexico and the recently-acquired territory of New Mexico, spoke some Spanish. "Don' know. 'Pears to be somethin' religious-like."

Clyde was still as he fingered his beloved whip. "I need to wet my whistle." He looked around.

More people, mostly women and young children, had emerged from their houses to witness the arrival of the outsiders. Most popped back inside; a few remained to see what might happen.

Bert, who had ignored Clyde's desire for drink, asked, "Yeah, Whitey, what you figure's goin' on?" He stared at the distant scene, visible through the clearing made by the central road in and past the separation between houses.

"Hell, some sorta' religious shit." He waved his hand impatiently.

T.J., who rested his arms on his saddle pommel, pushed his hat back on his head and grinned. "Hey, Clyde, why don't you go up there an' pray with 'em?"

All but Clyde and Barney laughed as Clyde dismounted and lead his horse to the hitching rail in front of the *tienda*.

Barney looked up at the crude sign over the door to the building. It read, "TIENDA Y CANTINA." He mouthed the words he didn't understand, then followed suit as the others emulated Clyde's action.

They all dismounted, threw the reins of their horses around the thin pine rail, and entered the building single-file. Barney was slow, but followed with grudging trepidation in his steps.

Chet was last. After securing his mount, and before entering, he stopped, turned and looked toward the house where young Gloria had disappeared after her shock. He swallowed hard, then followed the others into the store.

The *tienda* was the largest building in the village. It was situated near the entrance to the settlement along the horse and wagon-rutted road that connected it with the river valley to the west. Its high, thick adobe walls lent it a cavernous appearance. The sole exterior light came through two narrow windows which faced the dirt street beyond a simple, narrow, uncovered plank approach. That, in turn, sported a broken piece of cast-iron plow share on one edge for the scraping of boot and shoe soles. The interior walls were white-washed with *yeso*, which served to reflect a little more light than otherwise. Those were lined with shelves that reached from the hand-finished pine plank floor to the thick *viga*-supported ceiling. They held bottles, jars, pots, pans, sacks, small and medium-sized wooden and pasteboard boxes, candles, lanterns, paper-wrapped soaps and the like. Along the center were barrels and crates, some of which held grain, corn, beans, rakes, hoes, shovels and other farm and garden implements. One area, near the door, featured a rack which offered a meager amount of local fruits and vegetables.

Three oil lamps descended from the ceiling. One, near the back of the big room, the darkest part, was lit. It shone on a make-shift bar of hand-adzed local pine plank. It was supported by large barrels behind a big rectilinear table with benches along opposing sides. Below it, on the floor in front of the table, was a large cast-iron stove of the latest design. Its black flue rose straight up through the ceiling. There was no fire on the grate, a decision based upon the on-going village activities. Behind and above the bar was a shelf which displayed a poor selection of alcoholic beverages in crockery jugs and opaque bottles. There was no mirror.

Clyde was in the lead as the gringos entered the combination store, bar and sometime limited menu café, offered principally for the occasional traveler. They moved slowly, partly in their suspicious nature, partly to inspect the place and its goods, which they all regarded as amazing, given where they were.

With his beloved whip coiled about his shoulder and under his arm, Clyde rubbed his hands against the cold room. He glanced at the others behind him, then rounded the stove for the table and the closest bench, where he sat and continued to rub his hands after he placed the whip on the table.

It was then that Tomás entered the room in response to the sound made by the men's boots that drummed on the fancy plank floor. Middle-aged, with a bit of a belly and a full head of hair over a florid face, he wore a cloth apron tied around his middle. He wiped his hands as he looked over the small assemblage. His smile modified quickly to a nervous grin when he realized who his patrons might be.

Clyde looked up at the merchant as he continued to exercise his cold hands, then stopped to make the drinking sign with his thumb to his mouth. "Somethin' to drink," he said. "Pool-kay. Hell, whatever you got here." He awarded Tomás a severe, intolerant look, then turned his head as though disgusted and plunked his hat onto the table with a flourish.

Tomás halted at the end of the make-shift bar, swung his head around and moved his eyes quickly to judge his customers and process the possible problem that lay ahead. He looked at Clyde and nodded emphatically. "*Sí, señor*. Good morning. *Yo entiendo*. Understand. Please, be seated. I will serve you." He waved both his arms as a welcome sign. He then found a match behind the bar, pulled down an oil lamp that hung over it, and lit the wick. It brightened the room to a minor degree.

By this time, Bert, Whitey and T.J. had arrived at the table and each assumed a position on the bench facing Clyde. Chet, last to come inside, was at the front of the big, merchandise-laden room, where he closed the outer door with a clatter.

Barney, ever the self-appointed outsider, occupied himself with a cursory inspection of the myriad of goods on the shelves and scattered about the floor. He stopped, looked over at the others, then went to one of the two windows that faced the street, leaned forward and peered out. He was uncomfortable, but attached to his trail partners.

Clyde, impatient, rose, grabbed his whip and started to pace around the room. He slapped his palm with the whip handle as he cocked his head one way then another as he pretended to study the merchandise.

Tomás, who had gone behind the bar, returned with crockery mugs and a large wicker-covered earthenware jug, which he placed on the long table with care. He then backed away and forced himself to look at each of the seated gringos in turn as they helped themselves to the hard liquor noisily and without regard to spillage. As he smiled nervously, he wiped his hands in the apron bound to his waist, an unnecessary move, since his hands did not require cleaning. After a pause, he said, "Eat? Food?" He smiled and nodded as he made the gesture for eating.

The arrogant men ignored him and continued to pour drinks from the big jug.

It was then that Chet arrived, sat, reached for a mug and helped himself to a large portion of the fermented cactus juice.

Barney arrived and took a seat next to Chet, who was alongside Clyde's position. "I gotta' eat 'afore I guzzle." He swiped at his errant red hair. He had no plan to drink, but made the remark to bring up the question of food.

"I could eat," Chet declared.

Whitey looked up at the expectant Tomás. "Uh, sí, Uh, *desa—*"

Tomás smiled more easily, happy to hear some Spanish. "*¡Sí! ¡Desayuno!*" He turned and scurried away.

Clyde, finished with his inspection tour, returned to the table, where he moved a small wooden barrel close to one end and sat. He rested the whip on the top of the barrel, then moved his hat there. T.J. passed the jug and a mug to him. He poured, then drank deeply.

Barney got up and moved across the room to avoid drinking before the arrival of the food and being pestered by T.J. for not partaking.

T.J. Looked at Whitey. "What'd you tell 'im?"

Whitey removed his mug from his lips long enough to answer, "Breakfast."

T.J. slurped his drink, then wiped his mouth with his sleeve as he winced. "Gawd!" he shouted.

Through the open door to the innards behind the bar, they heard Tomás. "*¡Amelia! ¡Tenemos huespedes! ¡Nesesitan desayuno para seis, y pronto!*" A moment later, he poked his head past the door. "*Minutos, señores.* Little while." Then he ducked back out of sight.

Whitey, the only one to understand Tomás, nodded blankly. Secretly, he felt a connection with the proprietor, but was fearful of disapproval from his comrades, who looked down upon Hispanics.

Chet removed a large hunting knife from its scabbard and began to carve his initials in the table top.

Barney, who continued to pace, moved back to a street-side window. He returned with enthusiasm after he turned to see Tomás come to the table with a plate of tortillas and a large bowl of beans. A few seconds later, he had plates, bowls and utensils on the table as well.

Chet and T.J. were obviously woozy as they reached for food.

Chet shouted, "Hey! How'er we supposed to eat this shit?!"

Whitey answered quietly, "With these. The tor-tee-ahs." He stretched the word out. "Like this." He tore off a piece of the thick, white flat bread, folded it into a scoop, and maneuvered beans onto it and shoved it into his mouth.

Tomás stepped back, folded his hands across his ample belly, and proclaimed, *¡Desayuno, señores!* I hopes it good! You enjoy! I bring more."

He was ignored by all as they dug in ravenously, Barney chief among them, who behaved as though he had never eaten before.

Tomás backed away slowly until he stood against the bar, watched tentatively for a moment, then retreated to the room behind the store area. A few seconds passed before Tomás' wife poked her head around the doorframe, looked for a moment, then as quickly disappeared.

The gringos did not notice.

4

On *Calvario*, the procession had reached the place where the two widely-separated "criminal" crosses were in place.

Polito, in front of his two tortured associates, had struggled to place the heavy wooden cross he had dragged from the village into the hole dug for it. Three sympathetic people, two men and a *reboso*-covered woman, unable to watch with inaction, had come to his aid. They were followed by Nicanora, his wife. Together with Polito, dispite the *Penitente* brothers, especially the *Hermano Mayor*, who silently objected, they had succeeded in placing the cross upright. That was followed by the ritual of the brothers packing dirt around the base then lifting Polito into place on the cross, where they bound him with horsehair rope. The thorn ring remained in place on his bloody head, below which his body was cut and scraped, red and purple with bruises from the torture he had endured.

At the same time, the other two men had been also lifted into place and bound on their respective crosses.

All three faux victims had pain and suffering written on their wracked faces; more so Polito, who had been beaten the worst of the three. As a result, he was barely aware of the reverential people gathered below him.

That included Nicanora, whose face was tear-streaked as she spoke in a whisper to herself after biting her lip. "Oh, God help you my husband."

It was then that a brief, gentle flurry of light snow flakes swirled around the crosses and moved the *rebosos* and ponchos of the faithful.

In the *cantina*, Tomás stood behind the bar as he wiped glasses and kept an anxious eye on the gringos at the table. A pork stew laced with green chile, diced potatoes and onions had been added to the proffered fare, and the trail-dusty gringos feasted. Despite the food, all but Barney were in their cups from imbibing the potent liquor.

T.J. sat back, rubbed his midriff, emitted a loud, proud belch, then stared at young Barney. "Say there, Barney, now you've stuffed yore gut, yew can be sociable." He shoved his cup, half full of *aguardiente*, in the boy's direction.

Barney looked up from his victuals, finished chewing, then swallowed. With a spoon in his hand, he shoved the cup away such that it tipped, rolled, and spilled its fiery contents onto the table. "You drink it! Git yoreself stinkin' fer all I care!" He returned to his fundamental task, hunched over the food in front of him.

T.J. pointed his finger at Barney as he started off the bench in a threatening pose. "Hey, boy! You watch yore tongue with me!"

Bert looked at T.J., then spoke quietly as he attempted to mellow the situation. "Leave 'im be, T.J. He don't have to drink if he don't want."

T.J sat down, lowered his head and awarded Bert a sullen look, then glared at Barney, who had resumed his breakfast with gusto. Clyde looked from T.J., to Bert, then Barney with sinuous, calculating eyes, but said nothing.

Barney set his spoon aside and looked at Whitey. "Hey, Whitey, think you could ask 'im fer some water?"

"Sure," Whitey responded.

Chet, bent over his bowl, turned his head to look at Barney. "You don't wanna' drink none 'o their water, son."

Whitey turned to look at Tomás, who had become increasingly nervous over the outbursts at the table. He pointed at the red head. *"Agua. Para el."*

Tomás brought a pitcher and a cup to the table, poured, then stepped back.

Barney drank with slurps and drizzles as though he were dying of thirst, then emitted a loud sigh as he wiped his mouth and chin with his sleeve. He resumed his attack on the basic fare.

Clyde, who had finished eating, picked up his whip and fingered it as he stared up at Tomás. Tomás, aware of Clyde's gaze, took another step away and avoided the gringo's eyes.

Clyde waited a beat, then, as he jerked his thumb over his shoulder, he asked, "How come you ain't up there with the rest 'o them greasers?" He nodded his head insolently.

Tomás had no idea what Clyde had said, and looked to Whitey with a question on his pained face.

Whitey looked to the ceiling for words, then at Tomás. "Uh—por kay no *con estas*—uh—*los otros*? A-yah."

Tomás nodded vigorously. *"Ah, sí."*

Clyde growled, "Ah see, ah see! Is that all this dumb mex can say?!"

Clyde had interrupted Tomás. Whitey, Bert and Barney were not amused, but T.J. and Chet were. They laughed and roved their eyes about for acquiescence.

Unaware of Clyde's slur, Tomás continued, "Eh, the mountain. *Sí. Son los Penitentes.* They very—how you say—*religioso.*" He nodded with a weak smile as he looked at each of the six men in turn.

"Religious. Religious. Sure," Whitey said. He nodded.

"They—*los*—*El Cristo.* You know?" Tomás bent forward, his eyes wide. *"Sobre el cruz.* Cross. *El cruz del Cristo."* He spread his arms out, dipped his head to his chest and closed his eyes in imitation of the crucified Christ. Then he recovered, looked around and nodded his head emphatically with a broad smile. He believed he had won over the gringos seated before him. He went on, "They beat. You know—beat, beat—" He executed a whipping motion with a grimace as he did.

All but Clyde watched Tomás, fascinated, while he looked away and sneered in contempt.

"All the years. *Cada año.* They do this." Tomás continued to nod.

"Cada año. Every year," Whitey said.

"Well, what the hell is it?" T.J. asked.

Whitey glanced at T.J., then turned his eyes back to Tomás. "He says those folks 'er doin' what was done to Jesus. They go through it every year. Easter time."

"The crucifixion. Stations of the cross. Somethin' like that," Bert put in.

"Yeah. Right." Whitey nodded to Bert.

Tomás nodded again and smiled, more relaxed.

"No shit," Clyde said. "Why ain't he up there?" He fingered his whip and stared at the table top.

Whitey thought for a moment, then looked up at Tomás. *"Eh— porqué no está con ellos?"*

"¿Con ellos?"

Tomás held his palms out in a gesture of denial. *"¡Es secreto! Solamente los penitentes. ¡Es para los otros! No señor. No soy penitente."* He swung his head back and forth emphatically.

Clyde looked up at Tomás, then at Whitey, his impatient irritation showing. "What the hell was that about?!"

"Says it's secret," Whitey answered.

Barney, sated, who sensed trouble looming, got up slowly and returned to one of the street windows and looked out.

Clyde stood, wobbled for a moment, jammed his hat on at a crazy angle, picked up his whip and turned to look at Barney at the window. Then he raised the whip and lashed it out across the room. Some of the shelved tins fell to the floor as the tip twirled wildly.

Tomás stepped back in horror. Barney turned to look as the others reacted.

A chorus of gringo voices shouted, "Hey! Why the hell you do that?! What'er you doin?!" There were joyful smiles and insincere frowns.

Tomás retreated behind the bar.

Bert thought for a moment, then stood. "What'er you doin' Clyde?! He frowned and held out his hands in a question.

Clyde ignored Bert and gathered the whip in. "Showin' the Mex," he muttered. He turned to look at Tomás who cowered behind the bar, then squared himself up and popped the whip again. He aimed in a different direction, and more jars, tins, cups and pasteboard boxes fell from shelves to the floor. A crockery jar of honey broke open and a box with a white powder split. The contents ran together to make a gooey white and golden mess on the plank floor.

Chet and T.J. both stood to watch the action and both, to be allied with Clyde, laughed disingenuously. T.J. looked toward the terrified Tomás to guage his reaction. Barney, who remained at a window, looked back and smiled instinctively.

Tomás moved from behind the bar to the end near the door to the rear. "Please! Please! Go out! Please!" His hands were clasped in front of his chest, his head to one side, a deep frown on his jowly face. He then made the mistake of going up to Clyde in the central aisle of the store.

Tomás' wife, aware of the commotion, came to the door, took one look, placed both hands to her head and shrieked. Bert reacted quickly, swung around with his Colt's .44 out and pointed in the direction of the noise. He looked at her for a moment, his eyes wide, frozen, then holstered his weapon. He shook his head, sighed and looked down as he holstered his gun.

The other men who remained at the table, but standing, laughed at the scene.

T.J. went into a crouch, made his hand into the image of a pistol, and pointed it at the woman, who had gone silent with Bert's reaction, transfixed as she stared at Bert's gun. "What's a' matter, Bert? Scared she's gonna' getcha'?"

That provoked more laughter, although not from Clyde, busy with his destructive rampage.

He turned toward Tomás, took three paces back, prepared the whip, then threw it out at the hapless man so that it wrapped around his middle and seized both his arms. Tomás, his mouth open in speechless fear, tried to pull away to no avail as Clyde reeled him in. Helpless and off balance, he stumbled and nearly fell as Clyde pulled him.

There was shocked silence in the great room as all watched Clyde and Tomás.

T.J., his voice moderated, given that he knew what Clyde was doing could lead to real trouble, something that, despite his loud bravado, he wanted to avoid, asked, "Hey, Clyde, whatcha' gonna do with 'im?"

Clyde tilted his head to one side; his mouth an insolent slit. "Well, now, you know, he ain't a very good citizen, is he?" He paused, then, "Now I think he oughta' be like the rest 'o them greasers up there. Religious like."

Bert frowned and smiled simultaneously. "Clyde—!"

Clyde ignored Bert and proceeded to pull, then push, Tomás toward the front door. Chet rushed past the astonished Barney to open it, and Clyde forced the frightened proprietor onto the short, wooden uncovered porch, then out onto the dirt street, where he spun and stumbled as he tried to stay upright. Behind them, the others, half drunk, followed. Barney, sober, was the last. He left the door ajar.

Tomás, still caged in Clyde's long whip, twisted half way when Clyde pulled on it again. When the whip ran out, with his feet crossed, he stumbled free, then fell to the ground, face down. Clyde re-coiled the whip and began to circle the downed man, who was too frightened to move.

As Tomás' porcine wife came out of the *tienda*, followed by a small frightened, sobbing child, a few villagers who heard the racket, came to their doors. Some ventured a few feet into the otherwise empty street. Old Santo also came to his door, then stepped beyond a few feet to watch. He was joined by his eight year-old grandson, who stood close to him and held his hand.

Clyde, who ignored the woman and the wailing child, continued to torment Tomás by lashing out at him, intentionally missing each time as the tip raised puffs of dust. Tomás, in reaction, tried to roll away as his wife attempted, unsuccessfully, to aid him. She circled the downed, dirt-covered man, bent over with shrieks and sobs; her hands alternately stretched out to him then close to her tear-stained face in panic.

Bert, T.J., Whitey and Barney, tired of the activity and secretly embarrassed, loosened the reins of their horses and mounted. Chet started to do the same, then stopped and looked toward teen-aged Gloria's house, his eyes feral. He then began to walk in that direction. Some of the villagers noticed as he didn't follow suit with the others. They didn't know his intent, but retreated, some inside their houses, as the armed stranger strode across the street.

Santo, who sensed what might happen next, leaned down to speak to the young boy next to him. "Son, go up there and tell the others! Hurry! Go the back way!"

"*¡Sí, abuelo!*" He nodded, fear in his eyes, then turned and ran first along the front of the house, then dodged to disappear between it and the next house.

At the same time, Chet reached the front door of Gloria's house, where he stood for three seconds before throwing it open.

Across the street, Clyde took final aim and struck Tomás with the tip of the whip on his arm, where it ripped his shirt and drew blood. Tomás cried out as Clyde backed away, coiled the whip and went to his horse.

The four mounted gringos watched as Tomás' wife and young, crying son went to his aid. His wife knelt beside him, squealed, cried and raised her hands in a gesture of prayer as her husband lay panting in the dirt. None of the villagers helped, as they feared reprisal, and moved their worried looks from the man on the ground, then the invaders, then again at stricken Tomás.

Clyde, winded, breathed heavily as he mounted his horse and wrapped the whip around the pommel. He wore a look of superiority, his head high.

The other gringos waited obediently for his next move, lined up and ready.

Clyde pulled the reins as though to ride toward the river valley, then stopped, turned and looked across the village toward *Calvario*. He worked his mouth as he pondered, then shouted, "Let's git us some greasers!" He did not spur his mount, rather he clicked it into a walk as he sat upright in the saddle as though royalty.

5

As Clyde guided his horse at a walk along the narrow village street, the majority of the remaining people disappeared into their respective houses. Only one or two stayed outside. One woman bravely ventured over to where Tomás, his wife and son struggled to remove themselves from the chaos.

Whitey and T.J. followed Clyde at his rate, while Barney looked at Bert, who held back, then started out slowly as well. As Bert's horse stood still, nervously waiting for his master's command, Clyde, T.J. and Whitey moved abreast toward the hill beyond. Then Clyde spurred his horse to a gallop, and the three picked up his pace. Barney kicked his horse as well as Bert finally, with trepidation, followed at a trot.

In contrast to the increasingly sunny street, the house where Gloria cared for a very young child was half dark. After his eyes became adjusted to the interior light, Chet spotted the girl who cowered in a corner, her young charge wrapped in her arms. As he moved toward her, she was frozen with primal fear, her eyes flooded with tears, and she instinctively raised her free arm in defense.

At the same time, Santo, who had not retreated inside in reaction to the disastrous scene on the street, went inside, roused to fierce determination. He hurried to a back room, picked up a carbine that rested in a corner, checked the breach, then left through a rear door.

On *Calvario*, where the Easter ritual continued, the people, villagers and *Penitente* brothers alike, were gathered in a rough semi-circle about the three crosses that held the faux-crucified victims. They continued to chant an *alabado* to the piping of the *pitero* and the racket of the *matraca* as the *Hermano Mayor* oversaw the ceremony as he stood next to the center cross, book in hand. Many were on their knees, their raised palms together.

Polito, affixed to the center cross, had the appearance of the classical view of the crucified Christ. His wrists, ankles, head, and other parts of his nearly-naked body were bloody and bruised from the torture he endured on the way, and that which he braved as he hung from the wooden structure. He was white with cold and agony, nearly comatose, with his head flopped down and to one side.

Black-robed women knelt in prayer at the base of each of the crosses. One of those at the base of the center cross, was Nicanora. Polito was unaware.

Penitente brothers raised the litters that carried the images of the *Cristo* and the *Madre Dolorosa* high. The auto-flagellants stopped beating themselves, while some in the crowd wept with religious fervor.

Combined with the chant, the wail of the *pito* and the clacking of the *matraca*, was another sound that caused some on the periphery of the gathering to turn and look toward the village below. It was the sound of horse's hooves approaching rapidly. A few seconds later, all the gringos, save Chet and Bert, charged up the hill and into the surprised crowd that scattered like ten-pins. Some stumbled, fell and scrambled to escape. Clyde swung his beloved whip high above his head. He, T.J., Whitey and Barney gleefully hurled insults and taunts. Bert rode up at a trot, did not shout, but circled the hill to help drive people into a frenzied, frightened, scattered pandemonium. T.J. pointed his pistol at people here and there, squinted and pretended to fire, then pointed it skyward and lobbed a shot. The report from the pistol added to the general fear and confusion, which included the confused hectic horses.

The villagers scattered at a run. Most struggled to find an escape route through the meleé as they scurried in every direction. More often than not, they ran into each other. Those who escaped down the hill to the village either huddled together in the plaza, or hid in their houses.

Clyde rode near enough to the *matraca* wielder to snatch it from his hand, then circled as he spun the little wooden noise-maker over his head, while the other wielded the whip.

Santo's grandson had arrived too late to warn the people about Gloria, so he stood at the edge of the chaotic scene behind the crosses, aghast and frightened. He backed away and crouched behind a bush.

Clyde stopped to survey the damage he and his comrades had caused. He looked up at the cross where Politio suffered in unconscious silence. "Hey, well, lookie here at this! A gen-u-wine Christ on the cross! A Mex at that! Now, ain't that somethin'!"

Breathless, T.J. reined his horse in next to Clyde. "Yeah. A collection 'o greasers all fancied up fer church 'an no church!"

The other gringos, who circled their mounts about the sacred area, laughed and shouted insults as they completed the job of dispersing the villagers.

Santo appeared, nearly out of breath, as he approached *Calvario* from the rear, behind the crosses, near his grandson. The carbine dangled from his hand. Unnoticed, he dropped to the ground behind a hillock, put the long gun to his shoulder, and took aim.

As his horse pranced impatiently, Clyde, transfixed by the image before him, hung the stolen *matraca* by its leather thong on the pommel, then uncoiled his whip.

T.J., next to him on his horse, wore a nasty smirk as he realized what his trail boss was about to do. He looked from the cross to Clyde. "Looks like they didn't finish 'im."

Clyde ignored the remark as he prepared to lash out with the long, leather whip.

Nicanora, one of only a few of the remaining worshipers and brothers, most of whom cowered nearby, rose from her place at the base of Polito's cross and looked up at Clyde and T.J. "*¡Por Diós, hombres, dejanos solos! ¡Quitanse aca!*" Her *reboso* fell away from her face and hair.

Clyde noticed her for the first time. "Well, shee-ut! Look at this 'un!"

At that moment, Santo fired the carbine. The slug ripped a hole in Clyde's shirt on his right side, immediately below his arm, but missed his body.

Clyde shouted, "Jesus! What the—?!" He looked about for the source of the report.

Barney, who had come up behind and to the right of Clyde, said, "Over there, Clyde!"

T.J. jerked his Colt's from its holster, swung it in Santo's direction, aimed and fired. His horse danced in reaction.

Santo threw his arms up, the carbine sailed away, he looked briefly at the morning sky, then slumped into death.

Clyde, unaffected, concentrated on Nicanora.

T.J., proud of his marksmanship, blew imaginary smoke from the barrel of his pistol, then held it lovingly against his face. He wore a wild, gleeful expression.

Nicanora was horrified when she turned to look at old Santo.

Santo's grandson, wild-eyed, stunned and momentarily frozen, looked first at his dead grandfather, then up at his killer, T.J. Then he ran, almost blinded by tears, to Santo's crumpled body.

A few of the villagers who had scattered, but returned tentatively, gawked at the unfolding scene, but stayed back, close to each other. Most were speechless.

Clyde then unleashed the whip on Polito. The tip struck his belly and drew blood, but there was no reaction from the man on the cross.

Nicanora looked up at Clyde in horror. She held out her hands in a pleading gesture. "¡Por favor! ¡Quitanse! ¡Vetense!"

Whitey, who had hovered behind, spurred his horse forward, ran at Nicanora in front of Clyde, swept her up, and with her feet dangling close to the ground, galloped in a circle around *Calvario*. He howled like a wolf.

Clyde, who concentrated on the job at hand, stung Polito again with the whip.

Bert rode alongside Clyde and looked at him. His voice was controlled. "Let's git, Clyde. We've had our fun fer today. C'mon."

Clyde, transfixed with his feeling of power, ignored Bert. He lashed out again. This time, the whip wrapped completely around the staff of the cross close to Polito's waist. He then hooked the whip handle around his saddle pommel and spurred his horse back. The cross groaned, hesitated, then crashed to the ground. Polito, still unconscious, was pinned between the heavy timber and the hard, cold earth. Blood gushed from his battered face.

Bert, T.J. and Barney watched Clyde's action in pure amazement, while Whitey, unaware, continued his victory tour with Nicanora across his horse in front of him on her stomach as though she were a sack of beans. As he came around close to he crosses, he slowed, then stopped to gape soberly at the scene. He traded looks with the other gringos, save for Clyde, who merely stared at his accomplishment in triumph.

The silence that ensued was broken when Clyde, unannounced, wheeled his horse around and sped off at a dust-raising gallop. The others followed with Whitey in the rear with his captive.

6

Severino sat in front of the pot-bellied stove in his small, chilly adobe house on the hill across from *Calvario*. His arms were stretched in front of him, palms out, to catch the growing warmth from the orange flames that shown through the little isinglass window.

Familiar sounds brokered his attention. He frowned as he realized he had perhaps heard three gunshots, two close in time to each other, then relative silence, then loud, unintelligible human voices. He hesitated, rose slowly and went to the window that looked out onto the porch and beyond. He saw nothing but the hill and the mountains beyond under the light of the bright early morning sun. He opened the door and went to the edge of the porch. With his brow still furrowed, he squinted in an effort to see across the little valley to the opposite hill called *Calvario*. He noticed what appeared to be odd activity; an unusual commotion, with people running, and moreover, horses where they should not be.

He returned to the interior of the house, donned his jacket and his hat, and, mindful of the slow work of the wood stove, closed the door as he left. He started down the slope at a quick stride, then broke into a run as he saw riders on horseback racing from *Calvario* toward the village.

On *Calvario*, several men and two women had returned cautiously to survey the damage. While the two "criminals" were un-bound and released to be lead away, limping, others struggled to turn over the heavy cross that held Polito against the ground. That required raising the horizontal bars high enough to allow the staff to rotate completely around. With the help of two more men, the cross was heaved over such that Polito faced up. The rescuers stood and looked, awe-struck, at the nearly naked, tortured, bloody man at their feet.

One man turned his head. He shouted, "Look!" He raised his chin.

Another man, who stood on the other side of the downed cross, followed his gaze. He frowned, his mouth agape. "Who is it?"

The man who had first looked, stared intently. "Severino!"

The other man said, "What?! Severino?! When did he arrive?!"

A woman said, "Oh, God! His brother!" She put her hand to her mouth, then pulled her black *reboso* higher and tighter around her head.

The man who had spotted him said, "He'll probably do nothing."

Another woman said. "I wouldn't count on it."

The men from the other crosses, assisted by others, despite their misery, stopped and turned to watch.

Severino ran up the slope, then slowed to a walk, then barely moved as he approached the raw timber where his brother lay, splayed out, still bound and unmoving.

The others, except for one woman, backed away to give hin room. They regarded him with skepticism. She, on the other hand, looked from him to his brother, then back, with tenderness.

Severino ignored the others as he kneeled beside his brother's body. He touched his head, then bowed his and made the sign of the cross.

The sympathetic woman leaned down to speak near his ear and said, in a near whisper, "Severino, they whipped him! They took Nicanora!"

Without rising, he looked up at her. "What?!" His voice broke.

"They took her away! On their horses!" She shook her head, then nodded.

"Who?!" He stood and looked down at her.

A small crowd began to gather around the flattened cross and the still body on it, as villagers trickled back to the catastrophic scene. Some had overheard the dialogue, which resulted in a chorus of voices. "Gringos! Gringos! A bunch of them! There were five! No, there were six or seven!"

Severino, in a state of shock, looked at the faces around him. His expression pained, he said, "Wait! Please! Only one speak! Who were they, and where did they go?!" He hesitated, then, "You say they took Nicanora?!"

Silence ensued, then the man who had first seen him approach, spoke. He was calm. "There were five." He held up five fingers. "A big one took Nicanora on his horse. Another pulled your brother down with a whip." He pointed toward the village, then back at where Santo lay. "Old Santo tried to stop them, but they killed him too!" He shook his head, then looked down. His hands were draped at his sides.

The woman who had pulled her *reboso* close, said, "Severino, he whipped your brother! He has killed him! You must do something!" Her voice was strong but pleading.

Severino stared at the woman, his face a mask of pain, anger and frustration. He looked at the twisted, bloody body of his brother, Polito, who remained, limp, on the cross, then knelt beside him again. He touched Polito's forehead again, then his sunken cheek, then raised his red, tear-brimmed eyes to look around at the people who stared down at him. He rose, looked toward the place where Santo lay, then went slowly to the body of the old man. He was followed by the man who first saw him approach *Calvario*. Severino stopped and looked down.

Santo's grandson stood next to his body and stared. Transfixed, he saw nothing and saw no one, nor did he hear anything as his sobs came in childish gulps at he tried to come to grips with the truth of his extreme loss. One of the women who had returned went to the boy and put her arms around him. She tried to lead him away, but he refused to move.

The man who accompanied Severino to Santo's body picked up the old man's carbine and held it out to Severino. He spoke gently. "Take this. Go after them, Severino."

Severino ignored him as he continued to stare at the old man at his feet.

It was then that a young man and several boys and girls ran toward *Calvario*, shouting. They were breathless as they stopped near the groups who still held vigil over Polito and Santo.

The young man pointed toward the village. He panted, "Hurry! They are gone, but there's another gringo, and they've got him!"

A boy who stood next to him shouted, "He was with Gloria!"

Severino returned to the group next to the cross. "What is it?! What are you saying?!"

The young man, still breathless and wide-eyed, his voice elevated, said, "Come see! They have one! They—!"

Severino looked severely at the young man. "What do you mean?! There is only one?! The others have gone?!"

Another boy stepped forward. "They rode away! The other remains! We have him! Come see!"

In the plaza of San Blas, most of the villagers milled about, singly or in small groups, as they talked amongst themselves. Some were loud, and demonstrated with wild, angry gesticulations. They were a clan, anxious to see and hear what was happening.

Severino and those who had been on *Calvario* with him entered the square slowly. They bore Polito's savaged body, and that of old Santo. The young man who had returned, carried Santo's carbine. With him was Santo's grandson, who wept openly as he held his grandparent's dead hand. He was flanked by the kind woman.

Some of the young people who had gone to the hill ran ahead as confusion began to take hold. With them, helped by other men and women, were the two men who had acted as faux criminals, and who moved slowly due to their wounds.

Severino received a mixed reaction. Most of the villagers had not known of his return. Many disapproved of him, while a minority did not. There were a few couched epithets thrown his way, while others shouted greetings. Sympathy began to grow for him among those who felt against him, given the events of the morning. As the delegation from the sacred hill moved toward the center of the plaza, the crowd hushed, then coalesced into two lines to allow the people with the dead bodies and the wounded actors to come forward and move across the plaza. The column then split, with part carrying Polito to his house, while the other moved off with Santo's body to his.

As the death procession passed, a lull ensued and the crowd merged behind it. Voices elevated as rumors began and people milled about once more. Some returned to their houses, while many, mostly young, excited at the events, remained in anticipation of more action.

They didn't have to wait long. Less than a half hour passed when the teen-aged girl, Gloria, and her mother appeared and were surrounded by a small crowd in the middle of a larger assemblage. Then Severino, accompanied by one of the men, a woman, and the young man, all of whom had been on *Calvario* with him, returned to the plaza as well. They moved slowly as the crowd quieted to a murmur and split for them. The young man continued to carry Santo's carbine. Severino stopped as he spied Gloria and her mother.

Gloria was bent over, her hands to her face, sobbing. She was disheveled, and a tore shown on the back of her dress. Her mother, a picture of vitriol and shame, and another woman held her close, in part to prevent her from dropping to the ground. Their bond broke as the attention of the noisy, undulating crowd deviated to another nearby scene. An open circle developed as the villagers stepped back to witness the new center of attention.

Chet had been dragged into the plaza, and lay on the bare earth, on his side, curled into a fetal ball as he attempted to avoid the blows and kicks of three men who attacked him. His face was bloody, his nose was broken, and his hair was caked with blood and dirt. He whimpered and begged to be released as one of the men struck him randomly with the butt of his own pistol.

A loud voice boomed over the cries of the people as the a path was cleared for the *Hermano Mayor*. He stopped, watched the beating for a moment, then shouted, "Stop! Stop!" He held up both arms. He held the ubiquitous prayer book in his right hand.

The three men obeyed and stood back. Their faces were masks of anger as they traded looks between the *Hermano* and the miserable, frantic gringo on the ground.

Pio, one of the attackers, moved his gaze from Chet to the *Hermano Mayor*, then around at the amazed, agitated crowd. He growled loudly, "Why should we stop?! This filthy gringo pig has violated my daughter! He deserves to die!" He threw his arm out in a violent gesture.

Some who stood nearby shouted agreement, while a minority said "No!" as voices rose and fell. Then all fell quiet in anticipation.

The *Hermano Mayor* lowered his head and looked at Pio. "Yes, Pio, you are right. You are absolutely right. But let us punish this miserable cur in the proper way. Into the jar with him!"

The crowd went wild as it shouted in agreement, and Pio's expression changed from anger to glee.

Severino, who still reeled in reaction to the events, remained sad and silent as he watched Chet being half-carried, half-dragged away, followed by villagers.

The gringo outlander, Chet, was taken to an open area beyond the last house on the northern edge of the village, near produce fields. There, a huge earthenware jar was buried in the ground with only a few inches showing. Chet kicked, shouted and sobbed as he begged while being muscled into the cavity, his arms tied close to his torso. His face was a mask of fear combined with desperate resignation. Unable to control himself, he vomited, and a wet spot appeared on his breeches.

The surrounding crowd went wild, then someone began to chant, and the *Penitente pitero* started his wailing tune.

The *Hermano Mayor*, his face a severe mask, stood near the jar, his prayer book open, as two men shoveled dirt into it. He recited something from the book, but his voice was drowned out by the shouts and taunts around him.

Chet lolled his dirt, blood and tear-covered head around as he moaned in panic and fear. Then he contained himself and pleaded, "Please! Please! Let me go! I'll pay you! Take my horse! Take my things! My pistol—!"

He was ignored.

A few of the villagers left the torture scene to form a group in front of Gloria's house. Among them was Severino and the man, woman and young man who had been with him on *Calvario*. They consulted in hushed tones.

The man said, "I don't know, Severino. They will kill you." He shook his head with a frown.

Severino looked at him without comment or emotion.

The woman said, "No! He must go! He owes it to Polito! And to all of us! He should go!" She shook her finger, stepped away, then came back with a huff and a toss of her head.

Severino looked at her emotionless, then started to walk away.

The young man said, "They whipped Tomás. He gave them food, and they beat him!"

Severino stopped and turned. "Who?!"

"The one with the whip."

Another man said, "The one with the whip killed Polito."

Severino moved only his eyes to stare hard at both men.

Pio then appeared from the direction of the jar. He carried a gun belt with a pistol in the holster. He held it up to Severino. "Here, Severino. Take this."

Severino looked at the gun belt, then Pio. "Where did you get this?"

"It is from the gringo. He no longer needs it. You do."

Severino looked at the deadly weapon and its holder for several seconds, then reached out slowly and took it from Pio. He dropped it to his side and looked away.

The crowd in front of the house began to grow as they watched and listened. Some murmured among themselves, but they were mostly hushed. Then, as though on cue, one by one, men, women and youths approached Severino and touched him or shook his hand. Some spoke quietly as they offered their condolences, while others nodded and made the sign of the cross. Two women kissed his cheek. One hugged him gently, then walked away.

Pio nodded sagely, then turned and entered his house where women were tending to Gloria and the child she had in her charge.

Severino turned, took several steps away from the silent group of villagers, and looked toward the west.

7

The eastern bank of the Rio Grande was sandy and laced with smooth gravel that had coursed along its flanks for millennia. Beginning a few feet away from the sometime muddy stream, up slope that lead to the steep cliffs beyond, grew reeds, willows, a few scrub oak, then cottonwood trees.

The afternoon sun was at the crest of the west bank as Severino rode his horse at a walk to the water's edge.

His saddlebags were full, and his bedroll was tied neatly behind his saddle. His military carbine was in its Indian scabbard to his right. On the left of the saddle was Santo's carbine in its locally made leather scabbard. On his belt to his left was his Indian knife; on his right, held by the extra belt with its cartridges ranged around its periphery, was Chet's .44 caliber revolver. His tasseled black felt hat was low over his eyes against the afternoon sun. Over his dark blue cotton shirt he wore his black leather vest.

He scoured the ground in the waning light. The soft, damp soil revealed impressions from horse's hooves. They pointed in both directions; north and south, as well as randomly. He clicked his horse forward, reined him to his right, then moved along the slow-moving river's edge, northbound. As he moved along, he dodged the branches of willows, tamarisk, reeds and other bushes that grew close to the water that flowed from the Rocky Mountains to the north.

He stopped to listen, then looked in every direction as well as behind. The only sights were of the slow-moving stream and the verdant playas. The only sounds were those of the motion of the water, occasional zephyr-blown leaves or the call of a bird. Below, in the sandy loam, more hoof prints revealed random directions. Those that pointed north were drier, while those indicating a southerly direction, were damp, or cupped water close to the river's edge. His survey and caution were natural. He was a tracker; a scout.

After moving carefully another twenty yards through the dense literal, he came upon a clearing. From the water's edge to an outcropping of shelf rock was some thirty feet. The gentle slope of sandy soil was devoid of vegetation. His horse halted and he looked about. Against a boulder separate from the shelf, he saw Nicanora as she languished against it. She sat upright, with her legs stretched out in front of her. Her torso leaned to one side, and her head was down on her shoulder. Her eyes were shut; she did not see or hear him.

He leapt from his horse, dropped the reins to the ground and rushed to her. He knelt down and looked her over before touching her. There were bruises on her neck, arms and one leg. The one on her neck bore the outline of fingers. Her feet were bare, her dress torn, the hem of which was high up on her bare legs, her hair disheveled. Her face was grimy, and there was dirt, mud, and bits of gravel and sand on her crumpled black dress. The *reboso* she had worn to the ceremony was not in evidence. She had been weeping, but her eyes were closed, and she breathed deeply as her chest heaved.

As he kneeled next to her, his face betrayed a mixture of anger and tenderness. He trembled as he reached out to caress her lowered face.

She raised her face slowly, then opened her eyes. She shook her head minimally and slowly as she mouthed something unintelligible. She tried to smile, but her mouth withdrew to an expression of pain, then to a tear-wet grimace brought on by crying.

When he realized her lips were dry, he stood, rushed to his horse to retrieve the canteen that hung from the saddle pommel, then raced back to her. She drank several sips, looked at him with sad, but loving eyes, then dropped her head to her chest and began to cry openly.

He whispered a curse as tears welled in his eyes. He looked up and away. . .

He wore work clothes, a straw hat and appropriate footwear as he labored to create irrigation rows between the lines of young corn plants.

She, in a flowered white dress, approached from behind Severino's bent over figure. Her hair reached down her back in long, brown braids. They were topped on her head with a flower she had picked moments before. She picked up a small clod of dirt and threw it at him.

When the clod struck him, he turned to see her tittering at him as she twisted back and forth, her hands clasped behind her. She smiled coquettishly from under her eyebrows.

He looked at her with a broad grin as he held his hoe to one side.

"Polito said I would find you here. Does he make you do this work?"

He grinned with a tolerant frown. "Of course not! I do it because I want to! I do it for my family. You know, Pablita."

"Of course. I know your grandmother, Pablita. She has made my mother's lace often." She hesitated. "When will you finish?"

He winked and pointed to the west. "Ah, you know, Nicanora! When the sun is beyond the valley!" He smiled.

She stooped to pick a flower from a small plant at her feet, then rose and looked at him. She smiled wanly, then turned to leave as she twirled the flower by its stem.

"Nicanora."

She turned. "Yes?"

"I've been watching you—"

She brightened, moved close to him, and manufactured a smiling frown. "Oh, you have, have you?! You'd better not let my brothers or my father catch you!" With that, she picked up her skirts and ran off.

He watched her go with all the enthusiastic anticipation a nineteen year-old boy could muster.

Four years later he sat, stiffly and alone, on a narrow ladder chair, but with a countenance of confidence and maturity, in the parlor of Nicanora's family home. His only companions beside the *furniture were two oil lamps that warded off the nighttime dark of the big room. His wait ended when Nicanora's father, Jacobo, entered. He stood immediately. He held his hat with both hands.*

Middle-aged, Jacobo had a bit of a paunch and was balding. He wore a cloth vest over suspenders, and his large, reddish handlebar mustache was slightly stained from the careless handling of soup and tobacco. He ignored Severino, who had extended his hand, as he walked slowly across the room to his comfortable over-stuffed chair. He sat with a puff and a grunt, folded his hands across his belly, then deigned to look at the young man across from him with hooded eyes. Be began to twiddle his thumbs.

Severino remained standing.

Jacobo finally spoke. "Sit, boy." He preened his mustache.

Severino regained his seat slowly.

"So, you say you love Nicanora and are prepared to provide for her."

"Yes, sir, I do." He sat forward on the edge of his chair, his hat still held with both hands.

Nicanora's father nodded knowingly, took in a deep breath and released it. "I wish your parents were alive. It would be much easier. There is the question of property."

Severino sobered as the requisite smile he had worn faded. He fidgeted. "Yes, sir, but I have—"

"Yes, yes; I know. The land on the hill. I know of that. But it is not the same as lower farm land, you understand. The sort that Polito has inherited."

Severino looked down at his hands.

"But you are a good lad, and I am certain you will be good to my daughter. You may set the wedding day."

Severino stood, as did Jacobo. The two men shook hands and smiled at each other.

Severino and his intended, Nicanora, strolled amidst the fiesta crowd. A few steps behind them was her aunt Ermelina, acting as her traditional dueña. The on again, off again light that illuminated them was from the myriad torches and lanterns set out about the plaza as well as the light that came from the houses that described the periphery of the square.

There was a crude, but colorful banner that hung over the open door of the village church that declared the saint's day. Most of the doors of the houses that surrounded the plaza were open. People streamed in and out, meandered about, eating, drinking, dancing, laughing and flirting. Tables had been set up in the center of the square for people to sit and partake. They were occupied primarily by elderly folk, who, as they ate, gossiped among themselves and watched the younger crowd.

Polito wended his way through the mass of people, a drink in his hand, when he spotted the couple. He stopped, sipped his drink, then moved toward his brother and his fiancé. The look on his face was not that of a happy party-attendee, rather that of intense anger. He carried two burdens; one a dire message for his brother, and two, the fact that he had hoped to marry Nicanora, and had been overthrown by his younger sibling.

He pushed his way through the throng until he was a few feet from the happy couple.

Severino spied his brother and waved heartily.

Polito acknowledged his brother's greeting with a curt nod.

When they were close enough, Severino tapped his brother on his shoulder in a fond greeting. Polito did not respond in kind, rather he gave Severino a cursory look and shifted his gaze to Nicanora. She understood the nature of Polito's look. Severino did not.

"Good evening, Nicanora," he said.

"Good evening," she replied. She blushed.

Polito looked at his brother. "Hello, Severino."

Severino, now sensitive to his brother's cool attitude, asked, "What's wrong, Polito?! This is a happy time!" He gave his brother a crooked, questioning smile as he held his hands out.

Polito stepped back, raised his head, and looked at Severino down his nose. "Not so for me. Because of you!" He pointed.

Severino tried to smile in a genuine way as he looked at his brother, to Nicanora, then back. He put his finger to his chest. "I?! What have I done?!"

Polito folded his arms across his chest, looked away, down at the ground, then up at Severino. He lowered his voice to a growl. "You have disgraced the family, and you have disgraced me!"

Severino nodded emphatically. "Ah! I now know. You think that because I refuse to allow myself to be lashed to the cross—!"

Polito leaned in and raised his voice. "You have been sponsored! You cannot refuse! It is a disgrace!" He flung his arms out violently, then swung his arm around and pushed at Severino's chest with his finger.

Severino flared and pushed Polito's arm away. He shouted, "It is a disgrace to wish to die on the cross?!" He pointed in the direction of Calvario. "My father—our father—died on the cross!"

Nearby revelers, now aware of the conflict, turned toward the brothers and moved in close. Some were delighted to see and hear the disturbance.

Polito, embarrassed, looked around at his neighbors. His demeanor changed as he tried to calm himself. He turned his attention back to Severino and lowered his voice. "Severino. Think of the family! Our tradition! Your father's name!" He held out his arms pleadingly, his expression intense.

Severino, agitated, shouted, "I also think of the name of my mother!"

Nicanora, confused, embarrassed and alarmed at the outbursts, shied away, her hands to her mouth. Ermelina touched her in alarmed sympathy.

Jacobo, Nicanora's father, learned of the shouting match taking place across the plaza, and wended his way to the conflicted group.

Severino went on. "I will continue to think of her sweet face at the grave of my father, and of his face as he hung from the cross on Calvario! You, Polito, are a fool!" He swung his arm around to point at the on-lookers. "And so are you all!"

Jacobo went to his daughter and pulled her away as she buried her face in her hands.

Severino looked around at the crowd that had become silent and watched him, stunned. He then turned toward Nicanora. He saw only her back as Jacobo and her aunt lead her away.

Polito closed on his younger brother. He spoke softly. "See what you have done? You have disgraced us. As the youngest son, you should be proud to bear the cross. But no. Not you. You will be fortunate if Nicanora marries you. You are the fool. I am not happy to have you near me. Pablita is right. You are different."

Polito, as did most of the on-lookers, disbursed, and left Severino to stand alone amidst the otherwise merry crowd.

Severino was angry, then sorrowful, as he watched Polito, Nicanora and the others abandon him.

He returned his gaze to injured and humiliated Nicanora, who had lowered herself to curl up on the bare earth. He got his bedroll, unfurled it, spread it out, and helped her onto it.

As the day waned, slowly, with gentle persistence, he was able to coax her to drink from his canteen. After washing her face and hands with water from the clear stream, he did the best he could to clean and arrange her matted hair. Soon, she stopped shivering, and she looked up at him.

He held the canteen to her lips again. "Nicanora," he whispered. "Nicanora—what—what did they do? Please, Nicanora, tell me. I—I can't—"

She moaned, turned away to avoid his eyes, and lowered her head. Then she looked up at the dusk sky as tears flowed to wet her cheeks again. Her mouth curled in anguish and her chest shook with her sobs.

He closed his eyes, shook his head, stood and walked to the river's edge. He threw his head back and his arms out wide in pure frustration and anger. He kept his voice low. "Ay, God help us! God help *me!*" He went to her, kneeled, gathered her limp, yielding body in his arms and held her as he sobbed uncontrollably.

He made her as comfortable as he was able on his bedroll, then gathered wood for a fire. With village-provided food from his saddlebags, he prepared a meal, a small portion of which she ate, then covered her for a fitful night after placing his saddle under her head and neck as a makeshift pillow. He held vigil as he sat against a cottonwood tree, a saddle blanket over his chest and neck, until the moon rose high enough in the east to cast ghostly shadows on their camp before he drifted into tempestuous, dream-invaded slumber.

Dawn brought a cool, gentle breeze that wafted along and between the canyon walls that cradled the long, meandering Rio Grande on its clear, then silt-laden journey to the sea hundreds of miles to the south. That, in turn, caused high, light branches of the cottonwood tree under which Severino slept to sway. As a result, a loose-fitting leaf slipped away from a terminal twig and sailed, twirling, downward to land on his face. Instinctively, he reacted by swiping at his cheek and nose to clear the mild irritation. He opened his heavy eyelids as his dream sequence faded.

For an instant, he thought he was somewhere near a river on the plains of Kansas; a familiar experience. Then, across the white sandy stretch of river beach, he saw the place where he had lain his love the night before. But there was something wrong, and for several seconds, he didn't know what it was in the fog of is waking. Then it came to him. Nicanora was missing.

He threw the blanket aside and stumbled, half asleep and unsteady, to an erect position to stare, then swing his head one way and another in an effort to spot her. As he scrubbed his face with both hands to awaken, he reasoned that she must have gone to find a private, hidden place for a bodily urge.

He went to her resting place, where the sleeping provisions lay in a tumble, then down to the river's edge. There, he saw bare footprints in the damp earth, small enough to be those of Nicanora. He waited and watched while he listened to the low, gentle sounds from the river and the surrounding foliage. Then, with deep concern, he moved slowly along the water's margin, the route of the bare prints. He pushed thick reed and willow branches aside as the flora became thicker. Several yards farther, he found a piece of cloth torn from her dress caught on a stiff branch. There, on the ground, the last of the prints pointed toward the river. There were none beyond.

Panicked, he called her name, then shouted it. He raced back to the makeshift camp site, saddled his horse, then moved as quickly as he could back to the place where he last saw evidence of her. He stopped, called her name again, then urged his mount into a gallop to ride north along the river, both in and out of the water.

Finally, he brought his horse to a stop, then dropped his head to his chest in tears. It heaved as he wept, his arms loose at his sides. After a time, he gathered himself and quieted, then looked up and shouted an oath. He rode back to where he had seen the prints disappear into the stream and dismounted. He found two dry twigs, created a crude cross with a piece of thong from his saddle bindings, then placed it carefully in the soft ground a few feet from the water. After a few minutes of deep reflection, he moved slowly back to the camp, gathered and re-packed his trail kit, then began a slow ride along the river.

He stopped, then guided his mount into the water, where he rode along the foot-deep water, first a hundred yards north, then a hundred yards south. Then he snarled another oath under his breath, spurred his horse into a gallop, and raced away, bent forward in the saddle as the disturbed river water sprayed high into the air with each plunge of the horse's hooves.

Well upstream from where Severino had seen the prints that pointed to the water, Nicanora hugged herself as she lay curled into a tight, fetal position. Her clothes were wet and clung to her frail body. She was hidden by dense underbrush several yards from the stream. Her eyes were closed, and although very cold, she was quiet and unflinching. She heard her former lover call her name, but did not react. Then she heard the splashing of horse's hooves in the stream as the man she truly loved galloped away, perhaps never to return. She did not cry.

She waited, drowsy, then drifted into merciful sleep, then awoke with the sound of birds. By then she was warmer, as sunlight had taken charge of the narrow valley, and her dress had dried such that it no longer clung to her otherwise bare body. She lifted her head, then pushed herself up. Feet bare and tender, she waded trance-like through green bows, then to the cottonwood *bosque*, then to the narrow, steep and rocky animal path that lead up to the plateau. There, she saw the outline of the village church steeples with the mountains beyond. Her bare, bloody feet hurt, but she was alive and didn't care.

8

The farmer was busy stripping a straight cedar branch to repair a breach in an animal pen. He stopped and raised his head as motion caught his eye. He dropped the branch, crouched behind the fence and peered around the end. He moved a few feet along the fence, grabbed an old sword that leaned against the pen and returned to watch the man on horseback ride into his yard.

Severino moved at a walk on horseback. He soothed his tired horse with strokes along his neck with one gloved hand as he spoke in low tones to the animal.

The farmer watched from behind the fence as Severino approached.

Severino spotted him. "Good afternoon."

The farmer rose, the sword held at waist level, pointed straight out, in one hand. "Good afternoon." He lowered the weapon until the tip touched the ground.

Severino leaned forward in the saddle. "I'd be much obliged if I could water my horse." He looked at the old hand weapon, then the farmer.

The farmer came out into the open, the sword still in hand. He waved it along the ground near his feet. "Who are you?"

"Severino Torres. From San Blas." He jerked his head in the direction of the mountain village.

The farmer relaxed his grip on the ancient weapon, then propped it against the cedar fence. "Are you alone?" He peered past the man on horseback, then up at him.

Severino glanced around as he leaned on the pommel. "I am. There is no one with me."

"Alright. You may water your horse." He pointed. "The trough is there."

Severino dismounted. The horse smelled water and required no coaxing. With reins trailing, he went to the trough.

The farmer said, "The well is there. Take water for yourself."

"Thank you." Severino went to the well, dipped water from a bucket and drank. Sated, he turned to his host. He wiped his mouth on his sleeve. "Why the sword?"

The farmer raised his eyes to the sky and held his arms out high. "Aye! I had the piss scared out of me by a bunch of whoremonger gringos! Holy mother!" He shook his head and looked at the ground.

Severino frowned. "They came this way?"

The farmer stared at Severino. "You know them?!"

"Five?"

"Yes, five! And one was swinging one of those—those long whips! We didn't know what it was. Scared us!"

Severino looked off into the distance. He lowered his voice. "It was them."

"Who are they?! How do you know them?! What did they do? Steal animals?"

Severino sobered and looked at the farmer. "Animals? No, they—"

"They stole one of my sheep! One of my best! At least they didn't come to the house and near my woman! She was out in the—" He waved his arms excitedly.

"Which way did they go? When?"

"Which way? Why, Santa Fé, of course! Yesterday."

"Yesterday? How do you know which direction?"

"The way they went. And they said they were going there."

"They told you?"

"They told me nothing! I heard them speak of it. They want to gamble and whore around." He paused and, frustrated, scrubbed his face with his hands. "You're not going after them, are you? They've got guns. I wish—" He paused again, looked at Severino, then the horse and the armaments.

"You do, too." He studied Severino, then said, in a near whisper, "You are. Yes, you are." He thought for a moment. "Look, come in the house. Have some food and wine with us. Take food with you. You look hungry. Food is expensive in Santa Fé."

"You speak English?"

The farmer held up his thumb and forefinger. "This much."

Severino looked off toward the south, then, after securing his horse, followed the farmer.

Santa Fé's mostly dark streets were a mixture of quiet and rowdiness. Most of the noise came from the town center, the plaza. The crazy-quilt of streets were also a mixture of private residences and businesses, many of which catered to fun, frolic, drinking, gambling, dancing and prostitution. The plaza was host to the busiest of outdoor activity, with groups either moving from one venue to another, or stopping to talk, shout, sing, smoke, drink, stagger, fight, stumble and fall. Most were men; some on horseback. Several wagons were parked willy-nilly, their tongues down sans draft animals. There were women in the mix; a few of whom were prostitutes. There were men in the blue uniform of the U.S. Army. Shafts of yellow-orange light aided in making the plaza and nearby streets navigable, while a few public torches strategically placed around the periphery of the plaza, made up the rest of the lighting. The strains of music that wafted through the meandering crowds were created by guitars, concertinas, violins, and the occasional castanet or drum. A rare brass instrument was heard by those sober enough to discern or care. The usual accompaniment was the loud human voice, both male and female, here and there, flavored with the effects of alcohol.

The principal saloon, the largest in the political and economic center of the territory, lay immediately off of the plaza to the west and north. The main room, with a sea of heavy, round natural oak tables, was crowded beneath a blue-gray haze of tobacco smoke. People, mostly men, with many of them in army blue, sat, stood, or danced with gaudily-dressed women, there to encourage the frivolity and the spending of coin and specie.

Virtually all had a drink nearby, in their hands, or to their lips. Poorly-rendered music that competed with the raucous voices of the revelers was offered up by a three-piece band dominated by an upright piano. Behind the long, well-staffed bar at the rear of the big room, was a large mirror.

Many of the men in civilian clothes wore high leather boots and laced leggings, drovers fresh from the Santa Fé-Chihuahua Trail. Their footwear showed plainly the results of that travel with mud, dirt and animal ordure. A number of the men in blue shared that distinction, having been with the trail columns as guard-mount. The locals in attendance tended toward more modest and tidier dress.

Seated at one of the tables were the five gringos, Clyde, Bert, Whitey, T.J. and Barney. All but Barney, who slumped in his chair with a dark pout on his face, had alcoholic drinks at their elbows. Although Bert, Whitey and T.J. played a game of cards, the table was covered by crumb- and scrap-scattered plates, saucers, cups and utensils. A waiter who wore suspenders and a long, white apron approached and unceremoniously gathered up the used dishes with a clatter.

Clyde, his mind elsewhere and his hat on the back of his head, surveyed the room with sullen, feral eyes. A half-full shot glass was in his hand. "Ah gotta find me some excitement," he growled.

T.J. slammed a card down on the table. "Hell, I'm real excited! Hee, hee, hee!"

Barney shifted in his chair. "It stinks in here."

T.J. forced a chuckle. "Shit, you boy, you. Why don' you find a place to lie down an' play with yore peter?"

The others paid no attention to T.J.'s remark. It was all old hat.

Bert sat forward and glared at T.J. "Goddamnit, T.J., you gonna play cards or jaw the evenin' away?!"

T.J. sobered and played his hand.

Whitey forced a loud belch.

Clyde straightened, downed the last of his glass, then held it up. "That does it, you dumb sod-busters! I'm going over to the lady's parlor!"

T.J. looked at Clyde askance. "What?! You didn't git enough at the river?!" He looked at his cards.

Clyde awarded T.J. a searing, side-long glance, slammed the shot glass onto the table, made a face, then scraped his chair back and stood.

T.J. continued to rag on Clyde, something he would not have done had they been alone. "Good thing ya' changed that shirt 'o your'n. That ole man up there shore made it holy!" He laughed and looked at Bert and Whitey for support.

Bert smiled faintly and Whitey chuckled. Barney closed his eyes as though bored. Clyde sneered and started away.

Barney said, his eyes closed, "His best shirt."

Whitey threw his cards down. "Hang on there, Clyde! I'm a-comin' with you! I need a little squirt myself after all these weeks, even if it is with a Mex!"

Clyde halted and looked back as Whitey rose, made an idle gesture, then continued.

T.J. looked up at Whitey. "Hey! What about the game?! This might be my big hand!" He held out his cards.

Whitey stopped to look back at T.J. He pointed. "I'll come back an' piss on them cards!"

With that, the two men exited the saloon.

T.J. stared at the cards he held. "Shit! You'd think after hoggin' that filly up north Clyde'd be satisfied!" He made a pouty face.

"Shut up, T.J. I call," Bert said.

Barney slumped more, then straightened, lurched onto the table and put his head down on its surface. T.J. swiped at him, then pushed his head.

Although nighttime with little light, Severino, wary, rode slowly into the outskirts of the town. He had been to Santa Fé before, but it had been more than two years.

Meanwhile, Clyde and Whitey prepared their mounts outside the saloon when Barney came bounding out.

"Hey! I'm a-comin' with ya'!"

Clyde muttered, "Ah don' know what fer."

Whitey checked his saddle cinch as he chewed on a small, sharp stick used to clean his teeth. "Sure, kid. C'mon along. Ya' might learn somethin'."

Barney went to his horse. "I might at that, by god."

At the same time, Severino had ridden farther into the depths of the town. He heard the sounds of revelry, saw people here and there, as well as idle saddled horses, wagons and men on horseback. Increasingly wary, he watched everything and everybody.

In the saloon, now absent Clyde, Whitey and Barney, Bert and T.J. remained, cards in hand and on the table.

T.J., normally full of bluster and braggadocio, scooted his chair closer to Bert. He looked around the big room furtively. "Hot damn, Bert, I swear I don't like all these blue coats around. They make me nervous as a cat." He peered at his game partner.

Bert sat back, took his eyes off his cards, glanced about the room, then back at his hand. "Aw, hell, T.J., don't worry 'bout it. If they suspect you'o somethin', why, I'll just tell 'em you're the one, put my hat on an' leave. Nothin' to worry over." He smiled at his own joke and moved one of the cards.

T.J. glared at Bert, then looked up at something that caught his attention. His focus was Tito, a scrawny little man of indeterminate age, who wore a seedy coat too large for his frame, a ratty felt hat and well-worn boots.

He worked his way through the noisy, smoke-dominated room. He stopped, licked his lips over his half-beard and looked about the room as though sizing it up. When he saw the two gringos, he sidled up to the table. He forced a smile. "*Señores!* may I join you?" He cocked his head submissively.

T.J. answered without paying the newcomer the courtesy of looking up at him. "Why? Cain't find a chair nowheres else?"

"Yes. But I would like to talk to you. You look very friendly."

T.J. looked up, his brow wrinkled. "Well, we ain't! So vamoos!" He jerked his head.

Tito, undaunted, said, "But I have a business proposition for you." His smile had tapered off to one more calculating and reserved.

Bert squinted an eye up at Tito. He took two beats. "What kinda' business?"

Tito felt more confident, and looked around the crowded room, then said, "Silver. Money."

Bert and T.J. adjusted their chairs, scanned the room for possible eaves-droppers, then looked at each other. Bert nodded to Tito, indicating that he should sit. The little man did so quickly.

T.J.'s eyes roved, then he looked at Tito and lowered his voice. "What's the deal?"

Tito cleared his throat, glanced around the room, then leaned in. He had sobered completely. "I would do it myself, but you have something I do not."

Bert, impatient, spat, "What?!"

Tito pointed emphatically at the table top, at an angle. He whispered, *"Pistoles."*

The infamous bawdy house established by *Doña Tules* was two blocks west of the saloon where Bert and T.J. remained with Tito. A large, two-story building, it featured a crib on the floor above the saloon and meeting room below. The street floor featured a modern pine floor, a bar with a back-bar mirror, paintings of women in suggestive poses, and games, such as monte, a favorite of the proprietress. A piano in one corner played against the hum of the crowd, mostly men; most of whom were well-dressed. A stairway lead to the upper floor, where most of the women were. Some of those not actively engaged roamed the lower area, soliciting business, seconding as waitresses, and sharing drinks with men who paid for them. As with the saloon down the street, it was noisy and smoke-filled.

Clyde, Whitey and Barney entered from the porch along the dirt street. They halted immediately inside.

Barney gawked at the room, his mouth agape. "Gawd a' mighty! What a place!"

Whitey rubbed his hands together gleefully. "Hot damn! Looks aw' right to me, Clyde! Let's git us somethin' goin' here!"

Clyde turned his entire body to face his companions closely. He couched his words. "Now, goddamnit, calm down, the two 'o ya'! Don't let on where you hail from, or you might git us throwed out! Let's find us a table an' sit." He looked around, then back. "Quiet-like."

Whitey leaned in close to Clyde. "Fer Chrissakes, listen to ya', Clyde! You sound like an' ole maid! C'mon, let's git us a poke!"

Barney turned away. "Well, I ain't lyin' down with no Mex!"

Clyde pointed his finger at Barney's chest. "Then you jest keep yore nose clean, boy!" He looked away, then back at Barney. He lowered his voice again. "Set down an' keep an eye peeled. An' have a goddamn drink! I'm buyin."

The Madam approached the three out-of-place gringos. She was over-dressed, overweight and matronly. She looked them over, then cocked her head in an ingratiating manner. "Welcome, gentlemen." She threw her arm out in a wide arc. "Come and sit. Relax. What will you have? We have everything here. Come." She turned to lead the way. "Here is a table for you." She made a lavish gesture with her arm outstretched and waved her ring-laden hand.

Barney looked at the woman as though she carried the plague, while Whitey and Clyde put on their best sophisticated behavior.

The madam stood by as the three went to the table she indicated. "Here we are. Please be seated. I will send a waiter." She swished away, collared a waiter, spoke to him, then went on.

A few of the better-dressed men in the room glanced at the new-comers, but soon lost interest as the three trail-dusty gringos took seats at the table.

Barney craned his neck to look around the room. "Shee-ut! Ain't this the fancy place! I never knew no Mex place'd look like this!"

Clyde looked away disdainfully.

Whitey frowned. "Jeezuzs, Barney! What'd you think it'd look like?!"

Barney, chastised, removed his hat long enough to sweep his errant red hair back, then settled it low over his forehead. "Hell, I don't know! Only places I seen in these parts was mud walls an' dirt floors."

"You act like you was born yestidday." Whitey leaned in. "Would you try an' look different? I mean, have a drink 're somethin.'"

Barney sat back and up, pushed his hat back, then swung his head around to survey the busy, noisy room again. "Aw', goddamnit, aw' right, but not much. That shit makes me dizzy."

Clyde, still in his private thoughts, continued to study the room. He broke his reverie to say, "Hope they got some good 'uns." He shook his head. "Gotta' wet my whistle first."

It was then that a waiter came to the table. He wore a bored look on his lean, dark mustachioed face. "*Sí, señores. ¿Que quieren?*"

Barney looked at Whitey. "What'd he say, Whitey?"

"Wants to know what we want." He looked up at the waiter. "*Aguardiente. Tres.*"

The waiter looked down his nose at each of the drifter gringos, then left without acknowledging the order.

"What'd you say, Whitey?" Barney peered at Whitey.

Clyde chuckled. "What he always says. That goddamn fermented cactus whoopie juice."

Whitey wobbled his head and looked around. He brushed imaginary dust from the table. "Well, hell. Whiskey from Kaintuck will set you back a goddamn fortune."

"That's fer sure," Clyde remarked. He cracked a wry grin and looked away. "But this shit makes ya' drunk faster!"

Barney looked up. "Sure quick here. Here he comes."

9

Meanwhile, Severino walked his horse along the dark, dirt street. Wary and uncertain, he looked at everything in general and nothing in particular. He was fatigued, hungry and thirsty, but not so much so that he was willing to enter a public place. He possessed little in the way of coin or specie, but did carry food and water from San Blas as well as that provided by the kind but shaken farmer and his wife. He reached into a saddlebag for a piece of bison jerky and began to chew on it.

As he passed the Tule saloon, two of the eight horses tied at the rail whinnied and moved about against their reigns in reaction to him and his mount. As he reached out along his horses long neck and made soothing sounds to quiet him, he looked at the rail-bound horses. He then spied something in the half-light that streamed from the raucous saloon.

He reigned his horse to a halt, dismounted, and walked slowly to one of the captive horses. He looked about to see if anyone was watching, then moved closer to the horse's saddle. Then he saw something very familiar to him. Hanging from the pommel with a length of leather string was a *matraca*, a *Penitente* ceremonial noise-maker.

As his heart pounded, he backed away from the line of horses and stood and looked the building over. He returned to his horse, lifted the reins and guided it around a dark corner of the building on the side away from the street. There, he looped the reins around the end of the rail as he spoke in low tones to the animal. He stood for a moment, silent, touched the hunting knife at his side, adjusted the gun belt, then started for the entrance to the building.

Inside, the three gringos had been served their drinks. Clyde and Whitey slugged theirs down, while Barney, who genuinely hated alcohol, sipped at his with a sour face.

Clyde set his mostly empty glass down and looked around. "Where the hell's that woman? I wanna' git on upstairs!"

Whitey, in his cups, gestured as he peered at the youngest of them, "No, I'm a-tellin' you, Barney, my son, I jest gotta' git me some fresh stuff like I had in San Antone once't. They ain't no better! Need to try it!" He raised his eyebrows knowingly and put his glass to his lips.

"Mebby so, but I ain't gitten' with no Mex whore. Yore sick in the haid." He thudded his still-full glass onto the table and looked away as though in a pout. He put his fingers in his mouth to lick away the liquor that had slopped onto them, then made a glum face.

Whitey shook his head in disgust. "Jeezuz, Barney, you sure gotta' lot 'a growin' up to do, boy!" He looked away then at Clyde. "Hey! Looks like 'ole Clyde's gonna' git us fixed up here!"

Clyde waved the madam down, then got up to negotiate with her as he removed his hat. He was far more self-deprecating than usual. He knew he was in civilization, and smart enough to know that simply being himself could lead to a bad end. He also knew he was out-numbered by a room full of armed men at the same time he wanted something he was unable to get simply anywhere.

He and the madam nodded in agreement as he put money in her hand. She walked away as Clyde returned to the table, his hat held at his side.

He leaned down to speak to Whitey. "All set, Whitey. She's gonna' give us the high sign when she's ready. Keep yore eye on that stair." He pointed.

"Where to?" Whitey asked.

Clyde used his index finger to point at the ceiling. "Upstairs. There."

Severino entered through the street door cautiously. He had never been in a place such as he witnessed now. He had no notion of what to do next, let alone how to act. He had no idea who he was looking for, but he reasoned that they did not know him as well.

He stepped aside as two men swaggered in behind him and nudged him against the wall. He held his hat against his midriff as he darted his eyes around the big room.

Whitey, who watched the stairway faithfully, said, "Well, I'm ready. Watchin' you with that stuff up north whetted my appetite!"

Clyde and Barney joined him in muted laughter. Clyde's was more rueful, unsure that Whitey had not slighted him, and glanced his way from the corner of his eye.

Barney stopped laughing, but continued to smile as he spotted Severino. He bravely took another sip of the dreaded *aguardiente*, then leaned forward against the table to look at each of his companions. "That feller just walked in looks like he's lost an' 'bout to pee his britches." He jerked his thumb in that direction, then returned his gaze to Severino.

Clyde and Whitey joined Barney to stare at Severino.

Whitey said, "Ya' suppose he knows what's on the menu?"

The three became wracked with laughter.

Barney sobered and pointed to the stairs. "Hey! There ya' go!"

Clyde and Whitey were deflected from the hilarity of watching a confused man by Barney's notice. They looked toward the stairway as well, then both rose and began to walk in that direction.

Clyde stopped, turned, and returned to the table. He reached inside his shirt, pulled out Nicanora's *reboso*, and handed it to Barney. "Hang onto this fer me. Ya' never know, I might not come back. Give it to my mother if I don't."

Whitey turned to see why Clyde had returned. When he realized what the transaction involved, he smiled, winked at Barney, then continued to the stairway.

Across the room, close to the entrance, Severino saw the actions of the three gringos. His first reaction was of idle disinterest, and was about to leave. Then when one of the men handed a piece of cloth to the younger man with red hair, still seated, something struck him; something familiar. The realization rushed at him that the cloth was a *reboso*, and not any *reboso*, but one made by his grandmother and given to Nicanora. Stunned, he watched as the two men climbed the stairs, looked once again at the man at the table who proceeded to stuff the cloth inside his shirt, then, nearly blind with fury, turned and exited the saloon.

Outside, in the deep shadows of the *portal* that fronted two sides of the building, Severino gathered his thoughts. His breath came in deep gulps as he stepped out into the dark dirt street, then moved backward to examine the big structure. He checked his surroundings again, went to his horse, and took the quirt from the pommel of the saddle. From there, he went to a large tree that grew close to the end on the upper porch. He studied it, checked the street and the entrance again, then climbed up and onto the second floor porch, using branches of the tree. Over the railing and in deeper shadow yet, he stepped back against the wall to gather himself. Then he moved carefully along the porch, aware of the occasional creaking of the floor boards, to the door that lead inside. He stopped, peered down at the empty street below, then, with his hat removed, put his ear to the door. He heard strains of music from the piano in the room below, mixed with voices that came from beyond the door at his level. He recognized both Spanish and English, but both were unintelligible. Some of the voices were more distinct as they came closer to the door. He tried the door latch, found it unlocked, and pushed it open slowly and silently. Ajar a few inches, he peered in to see three people, mostly in profile against the lantern light from the wall sconces along the hall.

He recognized the woman who had been on the stairs below, as well as the two men who had followed her, although he was unable to make out their faces clearly. He cracked the door open another two inches and watched as the woman guided the two men into separate rooms on the same side of the hallway, to his left. He continued to watch as the woman walked away, then disappear at the other end of the hall. He opened the door enough to slip inside, then pushed it against the frame short of the latch.

Fully inside, he attempted to control his hyperventilation as he crouched down against the end of a plush settee which was against the wall. He paused to get his bearings in the partial, flickering light. As he accustomed himself to the spare light of the hallway, he heard muffled voices and laughter from the cribs along the hall as well as banter and singing from the room and street below. Then he heard two louder voices, male and female, at the far end of the hall. A few seconds passed, then the overweight, out-of-breath madam appeared with a well-dressed middle-aged man.

She spoke in Spanish. "I hope you enjoy yourself this evening, sir."

Also in Spanish, the man replied, "Loretta has yet to disappoint me."

They stopped next to a door across the hall from where Severino hid.

"Here we are," she said, "I placed those rude gringos, those *Tejanos*, down the hall. They are always so loud." She pointed vaguely, then opened the door. "She spoke again as she retreated. "Good evening."

The man stopped in the doorway and looked at her. "I will be down later for a drink."

Severino waited until the door to the crib closed and the madam disappeared, then stood, calmer than when he entered. He studied the hall, then looked at the doors nearest him. He recalled the thick-bodied man who he had seen in the saloon enter the crib nearest him.

He swung his head about to scour his surroundings again, then satisfied that he was unwatched, crept across the hall to the crib door and put his ear close to it. He heard little at first, then a metal-on-metal creaking noise from inside. He looked along the hall once more, then opened the door carefully. He carried the coiled quirt in his hand.

Under the faint light from an oil lamp on a small table, he saw a narrow bed centered in the small room. There, two people, a man and a woman, coupled. On top, his trousers down, shirt still on, was the man who had climbed the stairs with the man who had transferred the *reboso* to the red-haired youth. He realized who the man was; the one the villagers had described as the man who had carried Nicanora away as though she were a sack of grain.

Neither the prostitute nor the man were aware of his presence. With the door wide open behind him, his face in a fierce grimace, he pulled his hunting knife from the beaded sheath at his side. He lunged forward and plunged it into the man's back two inches to the right of his spine and immediately below the rib cage.

Whitey arched up, removed his right arm from alongside the girl, and tried to reach around to touch the source of the pain. Severino pulled the knife out, then pushed it into his right side. As blood gushed from both wounds, the woman, who realized something was severely amiss, but unable to see what was happening, gasped, then reacted with a yelp. She tried to push the heavy, struggling man off, but was unsuccessful.

Severino removed the knife again, wiped the blood on the bed clothes, then slid it into its sheath. He then ripped Whitey's shirt up the middle, raised the quirt and struck the dying man's back three times. Bloody, purple welts rose on his soft, plump, fair skin.

As his chest heaved with deep gulps of air, Severino stepped back, stared at his work for a full second, then turned and walked from the room. Without checking the empty hall for witnesses, he went through the porch door, closed it quietly and made his way down to the street level with the aid of the tree.

Whitey, close to death and bleeding profusely, remained on top of the prostitute, his head alongside hers, leaving her trapped beneath his girth and barely able to call out. She was able, after several tries, to roll him off of her and onto the floor. Then she sat up and screamed at full volume.

Clyde, engaged as Whitey had been in the next room, heard the shriek, then commotion in the hall. It required five seconds for him to realize the source of the woman's scream was the next room, that where the madam had placed his partner, Whitey.

A few seconds later, the madam, although on the main floor, the saloon, heard the ruckus above. She headed for the stairs as fast as her portly frame would allow, long multiple silken skirts held high. Other patrons, also aware, modified their behavior to listen and gawk as the room quieted in wonder. Some arose from their chairs and looked about, uncertain as to what action they might or might not take.

Barney, oblivious, the little tumbler of despised *aguardiente* half full on the table, was slumped in his chair, arms folded, his hat down over his closed eyes. He was unaware.

At the top of the stairs, and in the hallway that led to the cribs, the madam halted long enough to see several of the clients in the hall or peering into it from their room doors. They all faced the far end from whence the noise had come, and which continued to fill the hall with the sound of female desperation and fear. Some were half-dressed; some nearly naked.

The madam moved deeper into the hallway, then stopped. She shouted, "What happened?! Where did the scream come from?!"

A man in a doorway pointed.

The madam moved toward the noise as Whitey's whore, clear of the dead client, ran into the hall and stopped. She was naked and bloody. When she saw the madam and the others staring at her, she dropped to her knees and keened with one hand over her breasts, the other over her crotch. Wild-eyed and hyperventilating, and fundamentally unaware of her actions or that which had transpired, she cried loudly, then retched and dropped to the floor, head first.

The madam lurched forward, stopped and looked up and down the hall. She waved her arms wildly. "Get away! Go back to your rooms! Stop! Stop looking! Go back!"

The patrons and prostitutes who had come to their doors retreated reluctantly.

Clyde, who had also come to his door, suspected that something serious had happened that might affect him. He realized belatedly that the frantic prostitute had issued from the room that he had seen Whitey enter. Despite the madam's demands, he remained in the doorway as he held his loose pants up under his wayward shirt. As the madam went to the girl, he hitched his britches up, tucked his shirt in and fixed his belt. His mouth hung open below his furrowed brow.

The madam leaned over and took the girl by her shoulders to raise her. "What happened?! Why did you scream?!" She pulled back as she noticed the blood. "What is this?! Aye! Did he hurt you?! What?! What?!" She recoiled as she noticed blood on her own hands. "Ayee! What were you doing?" She looked around in confusion.

The whore, calmed slightly, shook and cowered as she pointed to the open door of her crib.

The madam rose, went to the door and peered in. Her mouth dropped open.

Clyde, with his shirt partly out, his pants buckled, his boots in hand, crouched with tension over the cowering woman on the floor. He stared at her for a moment, then joined the madam.

The bloody girl forced herself up and joined Clyde and the madam at the crib door. All three stared into the poorly-lit room.

Whitey, naked except for his pants, which were down below his knees, and his torn shirt up around his shoulders, was sprawled out on the bare wood floor where the prostitute had managed to roll him. His boots lay beneath the bed. Blood pooled on the floor from his wounds. Clyde, in shock, half-whispered, "Jeez-uz Christ! What the—?!"

The madam turned to the girl. She whispered, "How did he die?! How did it happen?!"

The whore shook her head, her eyes wide. She stuttered. "A man! He came in—!" She pointed, arm outstretched, toward the hall.

"A man?! What man?!" She reared back.

Clyde looked at the two women in turn. "What's she sayin'?!"

The madam glared at Clyde. She growled in English. "He is your friend?! Your friend?!"

"Yes, but what—?!"

"Get him out! Get hin out! Now!" The madam thrust her finger in Clyde's face, then swung her arm around to point out of the room.

"What?! But—!" Clyde, totally flustered and confused, was speechless.

"Get him out! I don't want the sheriff! Get him out! Now!" She shouted as the girl cringed away.

Clyde looked at her with a deep frown and shook his head, his eyes wide. "How—?!"

The madam calmed a bit, then shoved the gringo back into the hallway. "I will send men to help. You take him out! Out that door!" She pointed to the door that lead to the second floor porch. She reached into the string purse at her waist and pulled out coins. "Here, take this money! Bury him! I don't want trouble!"

10

Severino held the reins to his horse as he stood in deep shadow across the street from the bawdy house. He watched as Clyde, Bert, T.J. and Barney gathered in the near dark next to their horses a few yards from the house of ill repute.

Tito stood a few feet outside the circle of gringo drifters. He watched and listened carefully as they spoke in low, fearful tones. In tune with the city and its denizens, his gaze included the street in both directions.

T.J. spoke. "Jeezuz Christ! I ain't never seen nothin' like this! How the hell—?!"

Clyde cut in. "They lowered 'im with a goddamn rope! Dumped 'im on the dirt! Fuckin' greasers!" He moved his head and looked about as he glowered in the half light.

"Off the porch?! Jeezuz!" T.J. exclaimed.

All four men became silent as they looked at Whitey's body draped across the rump of his horse. It was sloppily half-dressed and missing his boots.

Bert squinted at Clyde. "You say that whore saw this crazy fella just walk in there an' stick Whitey like a pig?"

Barney paced away, then back as he scoured the dark street. "We gotta' get the fuck outa' here!"

Clyde ignored Barney to answer Bert. "Yep. An' then he whipped him! Shit! Look at 'im! Them marks!" He pointed.

"What the fuck?! That's plumb crazy!" T.J. spat.

Barney stared at the ground. "We gotta' clear out. Rest 'o you don't, I will!"

T.J. Threw his arm out to point, and twisted his body. "Shit. The whore done it!"

Bert executed a half step toward T.J.. He pointed with his whole arm at the cooling body. "Yew sound dumber that you are, T.J.! How the damned hell's the whore gonna' do that from underneath 'im?!" He kept his glaring eyes on T.J. for another three seconds, then turned away and huffed.

T.J. turned away. "Shee-ut."

Tito, who had not moved, but observed and listened, said, loud enough for all to hear, *"Penitente."*

Clyde, irritated, moved alongside Tito, and leaned in to him with a sneer. "What'd you say?!"

Tito was unaffected by Clyde's aggressive stance. *"Penitente."*

T.J. looked away in disgust. "Goddamnit, Whitey was the only one could talk that lingo."

Clyde shifted closer to be in Tito's face. "What the hell'd you say?!"

Tito held his ground and shrugged. He blinked slowly. *"Penitente."* He folded his arms across his chest.

Clyde straightened, looked at Tito, then away, then back. "Well, what in corn-blue blazes does that mean, you dumb spic?!"

Tito, fearless, and with a tolerant smile, said, "The *Penitente, señor,* use the whip in secret practice. I thought perhaps—"

T.J. edged closer to Tito and Clyde. "Hey! This little bastard knows somethin'! I'll bet he knows who done it!"

Bert stepped up to Clyde, who had turned away from Tito. He glanced at T.J. "Shut up, T.J." He looked at Clyde. "You thinkin' what I'm thinkin', Clyde?"

Clyde, wild-eyed, his back arched with tension, stared at Bert for a moment, looked at Tito hard, then back at Bert. "If yore thinkin' 'bout that miserable shanty town up north, then you are."

Barney creased his brow and threw his arms out. "Hot damn! We been followed?!"

The gringos fell silent as they searched each other's faces with new thoughts racing.

T.J. broke the silence. He had sobered, and lowered his head. His voice was low as well. "I don't know 'bout the rest 'o yew, but I ain't plannin' on stickin' around here much longer to work out the details 'o this mess. I don't mind a good fight now 'an then, but with someone I kin see, goddamnit!" He placed loud emphasis on the last word.

Barney submitted, "An' we ain't seen hide nor hair 'o Chet, neither!"

Bert ignored these remarks, then spoke up close and in low tones to Clyde. "Listen, this here Tito feller says he knows where we can lay our hands on some hard metal money 'an other valuables. I say we follow 'im, git what we can, and clear out. Right now." He stepped back and turned away to look around.

Tito heard something, as did the others. He moved to investigate.

A small group of men marched along the street leading to the bawdy house. Some of their voices were loud, most normal, but they appeared to be from those on a serious mission.

Tito returned to join the gringos.

Clyde asked, "What about Whitey?"

Tito said, "I will help."

Clyde looked at the little man with unchecked suspicion. "How?"

"There is a man who will accept the horse and saddle. To bury your friend. Then you help me. You will have money." He looked at each of the gringos, unblinking.

They looked at each other, and each nodded assent.

Clyde pointed at Tito. "Done. You better be right!"

Tito ignored Clyde's remark as he turned to look toward the approaching men, then back.

"It is time to go. The sheriff, he comes."

T.J. said, "That settles it for me! We split up, I'll see ya' in El Paso! If ya' make it."

They all moved off into the dark as the sound of voices drew nearer.

Severino had watched and listened patiently from the shadows across the earthen street. He heard much, but understood little. Observing Tito, though, caused him to be not only curious, but suspicious. As the gringos and the local man left, he lead his horse to follow on foot, at a safe distance.

11

The sun shone an hour past the crest of the Sangre de Cristo mountains on Santa Fé's eastern verge when Bert, T.J. and Barney were ten miles south of that city. They sat their horses on the juniper-cedar dotted plateau that gently undulated and rose toward the steep escarpment that bordered the valley of the Rio Grande to the south and west. Their mounts, more or less parallel to each other and separated by six feet, faced north, in the direction of the city and the mountains beyond. Their saddlebags bulged with stolen loot from the profitable night before.

T.J. removed his worn hat and swiped at his hair. "Where the hell is he?" He spoke in a normal tone.

Barney, who volunteered to answer, said, "Damned if I know."

Bert, disdainful of his trail partners, looked at neither. Rather, he remained silent as he leaned forward, his arms folded across the pommel of his saddle.

T.J. squirmed in his saddle. His horse reacted by taking a false step and shaking his great head. "Wish he'd hurry 'an git here. I get jittery waitin', 'specially with the notion of the sheriff comin' over that rise."

Bert's voice was barely audible. "He'll be here. Now, shut up."

Barney reached into one of his saddlebags and pulled out a small, silver cup and fondled it. "Sure is a nice cup I got. Ain't sure o' what I'll do with it."

T.J., annoyed, reined his horse around and moved off several feet. "Give it to yore mother, you dumb plow boy."

Barney held it up to try to see his face in the shiny metal. "Ain't got no mother."

"Then give it to the next whore you fuck." T.J. spat to one side.

Bert craned his head to look past his shoulder at the youth. "Sell it or melt it down. It's worth somethin'."

Barney looked hard at Bert. "Damn! Bein' in that church gave me the creeps!" His voice rose in timbre.

"Didn't bother me none," T.J. growled.

Barney, tolerant, looked at T.J. "How much you reckon you got, T.J.?"

T.J. took his time answering as he stared at the northern horizon. "Shit, I don' know." He paused. "Only stuff I count's the spendin' money, an' I didn't come away with much 'o that."

Barney put the cup back in the saddlebag. He spoke as he did. "Well, I'm happy we didn't have ta' shoot nobody."

T.J. shot back with, "'Cept fer that pea-brained Tito."

Barney whipped his head around to glare at T.J. "What?!"

Bert, his relaxed posture on his horse unchanged, said, "Shut up, T.J."

T.J. rocked his head back and forth. "Well, we shoulda'. The little Spic'll shoot off his mouth 'afore we're outa' sight down river."

Bert unfolded his arms and sat up. He patted his horse's neck and scowled at T.J. "Don't be a jackass, T.J.! He's got more to lose than us. 'Sides, he knows some 'o the boys in El Paso."

T.J. turned his head away in a pout. "Well—"

"Yeah," Barney added.

T.J. awarded Barney a dirty look, an effort lost on Barney, who had looked away.

Bert perked up as he stared into the distance. "Hey!"

T. J. turned in the saddle to follow Bert's gaze. "One or more?"

Barney peered as well. He said, "One."

Bert said, "Clyde."

"How ya' know?" Barney asked.

"Way he sits his horse." Bert nodded, then re-settled his hat. He inhaled a long breath, then exhaled.

T.J., finally happy, reined his horse to prance a circle. "'Bout time."

Barney looked down, then up at nothing. "Sure gonna' miss Whitey."

T.J. spoke, almost inaudibly. "Yeah."

"Makes me think 'o Chet," Barney reminisced.

"Wonder how he made out?" T.J. pondered.

Barney looked down again, then spoke in a near whisper, barely loud enough for the other two to hear. "Sure spooky the way Whitey kicked. Reminds me 'o the inside 'o that church. Hot damn!"

Bert and T.J. both looked at Barney with alarm.

T.J. shouted, "What?!"

Barney continued, "Don't suppose the one what killed Whitey was the father 'o that girl he got up north?!" He looked at both with a wide-eyed question on his face. He tilted his head to one side and squinted.

T.J. stared at Barney, looked at Bert, then looked away, intrigued. "Shit." He spat again.

Bert stared at Barney reflectively for a few seconds, then looked in the direction of Clyde's approach.

Barney said, "Well, remember what 'ole Tito said about them people?" He pointed at T.J., again with a squint. "Hey, T.J., how'd you like it if some greaser laid with yore daughter—or yore sister?"

T.J. snarled, "Shut yer trap, Barney!" He wiped his mouth with the back of his hand, slapped his pant leg and looked away.

Bert darted his eyes around in thought, but remained silent.

It was then that Clyde rode up.

Bert looked at him. "How'd it go?"

"Real fine. Horse's re-shod. Done a good job." He took his hat off, wiped his brow with a kerchief from his pants pocket, then replaced it.

T.J. leaned forward in the saddle with a sinister grin. "Did ya' do away with that sneaky greaser?"

Clyde glared at him. "Goddamnit, T.J., it ain't necessary ta' kill everyone!"

Bert cocked his head at Clyde. "We got trouble with the law?"

T.J. lowered his head. "Well, I just thought—"

Clyde waved his arm wide and glared at T.J. "Jesus Christ, T.J., you don' do much thinkin' most 'o the time! That greaser did us some good, an' he might do us some more. He knows folks who knows folks. He give me some names." He paused, then turned to Bert. "Naw. He's gonna' keep an eye out an' head 'em off opposite if he has to." He clicked his horse forward.

T.J. pulled his hat off his head and beat his leg with it. "Well, I don' know."

Barney looked at him, openly pleased that he had been taken down a notch.

Bert turned his horse to follow Clyde. "Better git a move on. I don' trust this part of the country. That thing last night—"

Barney, who had fallen into line, muttered, "Yeah."

Clyde waved his gloved hand high. "Ah, shit! That was some fuckin' drunk stranger didn't know who he was killin'. Fergit about it." He clicked at his horse.

T.J. rode half a horse behind Clyde. "I don't like it none."

Clyde retorted, "There ain't nothin' you *do* like, T.J.!"

Bert raised his voice. "Let's git movin', dammit! I wanna' be in Alb' kirk 'afore we die of old age."

Barney guided his horse close to Clyde's and reached inside his shirt to retrieve the *reboso* that Clyde had entrusted to him the night before. He held it out. "Take this cloth back. Spooks me some to have it."

Without a word, Clyde took the shawl and stuffed it inside his shirt.

The four gringos rode four abreast, headed south at a rapid walk.

Barney, nervous, looked behind, toward the city, and roved his eyes over the undulating, juniper-dominated horizon.

In Santa Fé, although early morning, crowds milled in the streets surrounding the plaza and in it. Murphy wagons, horses, draft animals, soldiers, peddlers, Indians and local Hispanic civilians, male and female, served to make up a colorful, noisy stew. Most were bent on their own private business; others were busy offering something for sale; often directly from a wagon recently having come over the Santa Fé - Chihuahua Trail. Others sought something to purchase.

Tito moved quickly along the front of the Governor's Palace. He was feral in his outlook. Although he felt he was not being pursued, he wore the demeanor of one who was. It was his natural state.

Severino followed the little man a few paces behind, and closed on him. As they neared the east end of the long *portal*, Severino tapped him on the shoulder.

Tito, who feared the law, flinched in reaction and whipped around. "Hey! What do you want?!" He wore a deep frown over his open, fear-revealing mouth.

"I would speak with you," Severino said. He spoke in Spanish, his voice controlled.

Tito looked around, nervous as a cat, then at Severino. "Why?! Who are you?!" He shook his head in a rapid "no."

Severino also looked about. He detected no one interested in them. "Calm yourself. Only a question or two."

The little man relaxed a bit, then assumed the posture and body language of an insecure social outcast attempting to be in control. He straightened to look up at the taller man. "If that is all, I know a lot about Santa Fé." He tilted his head with a phony, manufactured smile and opened his palms in a giving gesture.

Severino looked again at the milling crowds. "Let us move away from these people. We can hear each other better." He guided Tito with a gentle hand on his shoulder.

Severino and Tito moved around the corner of the palace and along the east side of the building to a quieter spot with few potential observers. Tito watched his back all the way, then looked up at Severino when they stopped. Severino also scanned the area. He looked at Tito closely.

Tito, who remained nervous, asked, "What do you want to know? Looking for some pleasure?" His eyes displayed hope.

"What are you called?"

Tito frowned and shook his head. "Tito. Why?!"

Severino pointed past Tito's shoulder. "Who were the men who helped you rob the church and those houses last night?"

Tito stepped back in wide-eyed panic. He eyed the pistol that hung from Severino's belt. "What?! What are you talking about?! I am no robber!"

Severino grabbed Tito's collar and pulled him in close, nearly nose-to-nose. His voice was a hoarse growl, barely above a whisper. "Yes, you are!

And those gringos helped you! You tell me who they are and where they went, or I'll find the sheriff!"

Tito quavered and began to perspire. "Alright! Alright! Let me go!" He looked around to see if they were being observed. He attempted to smooth his grimy, wrinkled clothes.

Severino released his grip, straightened his own clothes, then looked around as well.

"How did you know me?" Tito asked.

"Never mind! Tell me!"

Tito shrugged and developed a silly grin. "A few coins only. A bit of silver. A few plates. Nothing." He shrugged, then threw out his arms. "They are rich! They lack for nothing!" His voice became a childish squeak.

Severino moved close again. "You little snake! I should get the sheriff, but I have no time. Tell me of the gringos!"

Tito cringed as he looked up at Severino with a deprecating frown. "I will give you some! Is that what you want?! I will share—"

Severino pressed in on Tito again. "You—!"

"No, no! Please! ¡Bueno! ¡Bueno!" He changed his strategy, his tone and his body language, to act as Severino's friend. He lowered and calmed his voice. "They are easy to recognize. One is tall, with read hair. A youth. A mere boy."

"Where did they go?!" Severino gave Tito space again, then scoured the street.

"South. To Albuquerque."

"When?"

"One—with the whip—his horse lost a shoe. I took him to the—"

"How long ago? When did he leave town?"

Tito shrugged and raised his eyebrows. "One hour?"

It was then that they heard shouts come from a short distance away at the edge of the plaza. They heard a woman scream, then two men shouted. Severino and Tito turned to see a small crowd of people. They were agitated, and a woman pointed at them. They heard shouts of "There they are!" and "That's them," and "The robbers!"

Tito looked at Severino, who had turned at the shouts, then raced away as the crowd began to move in their direction. Severino froze for several seconds, then emulated Tito as he turned and ran along the side of the long building. At the corner, the turned left and raced along the north wall, headed west.

The crowd, confused and raging, coalesced into two groups of men. One started out after Tito; the other after Severino. Two men ran for their horses. Since the sheriff or one of his deputies was not in evidence, the crowd became an impromptu vigilante posse.

Severino ran at full speed to and past the palace corrals, then to his horse, tethered immediately beyond. He mounted quickly, then spurred his horse into a gallop to disappear in the labyrinth of streets and alleyways between earthen houses.

A boy who had heard the ruckus ran toward the scene, and saw Severino as he escaped the crowd. Two men on horseback rode toward the boy on the east side of the plaza. When the boy saw them, he pointed. When they asked what he had seen, he merely pointed more emphatically.

When Severino reached the western outskirts of the city, and he saw no one behind, he slowed his horse, first to a trot, then to a walk. He watched his rear as he made his way through a stand of large juniper and ground-hugging sage. He looked once more before he dropped down into an *arroyo*. On the narrow, intermittently flooded flat ground, he dismounted and lead his horse on foot. Both banks of the dry creek bed were dense with sage, small cottonwood, greasewood and acacia. He stayed close to the foliage, with his head low.

He heard horses approach, accompanied by shouts from men. He removed his hat, then stroked his horse's head and spoke to him in a low, soothing tone. He brought the animal to a halt, then flipped the reins around a low tree branch. He crouched away and hid in the foliage. He watched as four riders moved along one side of the *arroyo*, single file.

Two of the men peeled off to move in another direction, away from the *arroyo*. One of the two men who remained at the gulch held a pistol pointed high. He spoke in low tones to his partner. Both halted and cast their eyes about, searching. Much of the confidence they exhibited when they began had dissipated. Ordinary citizens, they were not accustomed to chasing desperados.

One of the two men guided his horse down into the arroyo. He moved at a walk, then spotted Severino's horse, and reacted by reining his horse to a stop. He dismounted, then lead his mount toward Severino's horse. Frightened and nervous, he held his pistol out and ready at hip level.

Severino watched from his hiding place as the man moved slowly along, then sprang out and held Chet's .44 revolver to the man's back. "Lie down!" he whispered.

The man, shocked, hesitated.

"Down! Now!" Severino commanded.

The surprised man obeyed, and lay on his stomach. His revolver he held out at arm's length in the tan silt.

Severino knelt down beside the man. He looked around. "How many more?"

The man instinctively held out a finger. "One."

"Don't move," Severino said. "I am not the robber. You want Tito." As he spoke, he relieved the man of his weapon.

They heard the captive's partner call out. "¡Estévan!"

Severino whispered, "Stay here. Do not move!"

Despite the fact that his head was virtually in the dirt, the man nodded emphatically.

Severino shoved the man's gun behind his belt line, then crouched away, his pistol at the ready, along the edge of the dry stream bed. When the second man wheeled his horse to back-track and look for his partner, Severino waited for him in the rushes. As he came close, the man from San Blas emerged from the foliage and pointed his pistol at the surprised rider. He held his hand out and spoke only loud enough for the man to hear. "Give me your pistol!"

Surprised and shocked, the man on horseback complied.

Severino stuffed the man's firearm into his belt line along with the other confiscated weapon as he pointed his own gun at the man. He looked around quickly, then said, "Ride into the arroyo! Now!"

Severino followed him down into the dry bed, then waved his pistol, indicating that the man should dismount. He understood what was next, so he laid down beside the first man without hesitation.

Severino went to his saddlebags, retrieved a length of rawhide binding, and returned to his prisoners. He leaned down and spoke to both in a loud whisper. "Hands behind your back."

They obeyed while he cut enough rawhide with his hunting knife to bind their hands. That accomplished, he removed their revolvers from his waist, unloaded them and laid both next to the second rider's head. He spoke in a low voice close to both prone men. "You want a man called Tito. I am not a robber. Look, there are your pistols. If you or your friends follow me, I will not hesitate to shoot."

Past the southern edge of the city, he goaded his horse into a gallop, then reined him in. He turned in the saddle to look north, and saw no sign of followers. As he moved, he avoided the rutted trail in favor of landscape that could hide him should the need arise. After a few minutes at a walk, he continued at a gallop.

12

The four gringos continued to walk their mounts along the rise before the steep cliffs that lay ahead. Three of them felt confident that they were safe, even from any repercussions that might befall them from their profitable night's work.

Barney, on the other hand, did not share their calm, and continued to turn to look back every minute or two. After five times scouring the horizon, he stopped and reined his horse around to face north. "Shit!"

Clyde stopped, looked at the red-headed youth, then followed his gaze. "What?!"

Barney pointed. "There!"

The other two men followed suit and looked as well. They all saw the vague outline of someone on horseback that bobbed up and down, then disappeared, then re-appeared, then was lost.

Bert clicked his horse forward. "Nobody we know."

T.J., who peered intently, leaned on his pommel. "Still don't know who stuck Whitey."

Clyde guided his horse close to Bert. "Hell's fire, ain't no crime to ride a horse. Could be anyone. 'Sides, he's a loner." He paused, then, "They'd have to travel in a bunch to do us harm. Better believe it."

"I don't like it," Barney declared, barely audible to the others.

T.J. pulled alongside Bert opposite Clyde. He looked over at the youngest of them with a sneer. "You don't like it! You don't like it! Why don' you run an' hide?!" He wiped his nose on his sleeve.

Barney, unfazed by T.J.'s remark, continued to stare without reaction.

Clyde turned his horse south. "C'mon! Let's git! No use invitin' trouble."

Barney watched as the distant rider re-appeared, then disappeared again, and did not re-appear after the usual period. Reluctantly, he reined his horse around to follow the others. He said, mostly to himself, "Oughta' bush-whack the some bitch." Then he spurred his horse.

The Rio Salado rose in the southern reaches of the deep finger valleys that marked the southern-most region of the Great Rocky Mountains. When there was seasonal water, it emptied into the Rio Grande near the Pueblo of Santo Domingo. As it passed the deep lava escarpment called La Bajada, it spread out into a flat plain where the stream meandered back and forth across ancient silt from the north and the east. Along its flanks, at times the soil was wet enough beneath the surface to behave like quick sand. Horses and wagons more than a few times became mired, and found it difficult to pull free without extreme effort.

When the four gringos arrived at the base of La Bajada that towered over the northern literal of the broad arroyo, there had been rain where the *rio* rose. Puddles of predominantly brown water dotted its flat feature for miles in both directions. From their vantage point, they saw areas with reeds, some with young willows, and others with mixed grasses. They discussed the possibility of their horses foundering and where it might be best to cross.

T.J. blocked the sun from his eyes with his hand. "What the hell's that? 'O'er yonder." He stretched his arm to point.

Bert rode up alongside him. "Where?"

T.J. dropped his arm and pointed with his chin without looking at Bert. "'Cross the crick."

Barney returned to the other three so that all four were lined up abreast. They all looked, but were unable to identify what they saw.

"Looks like a wagon," Bert offered.

"There's people," Barney said.

T.J. smirked and wiped his mouth with his sleeve. "Looks like lady luck done smiled on us agin, boys."

Bert turned his whole body to frown at T.J. "Now you hold on there, T.J. We spread ourselves pretty thin back there. I vote we keep 'a-movin.'" He rolled his head around to emphasize his point.

Bert didn't want Clyde's opinion, so he avoided looking at him. T.J. did, and looked at him expectantly, his head cocked in a question.

Clyde, as though in a trance, stared motionless, expressionless and silent into the distance. Finally, he spoke. "Bert's right. We gotta' stay righteous 'twixed here an' El Paso. Too many sheriffs, too many blue coats, an' too many Mexes." He clicked his horse forward. "Won't hurt to be friendly, though."

Bert shouted, "Clyde! Damn it! We oughta' ride around!" He rotated his head in frustration, removed his hat and beat his leg with it.

Clyde ignored Bert, while T.J. awarded Bert a triumphal smirk as he goaded his horse.

Barney, without expression, followed dutifully, while Bert hung back, then, with a deep sigh fell into line.

"Christ a' mighty! Bunch 'a locos!" Bert exclaimed. The others ignored his plaint.

A flat, Murphy-type wagon was stuck in marshy ground along the southern edge of the wide, meandering Rio Salado. Amongst a thicket of tall reeds, it was mired close to the downslope of the trail that connected Santa Fé with Albuquerque and points south. Under the wagon, next to a rear wheel, an unconscious man lay. One of his legs was under the wheel, broken. A pretty, auburn-haired woman in a long dress and her nine year-old son, both caked with mud, struggled to move the wagon to free the man, her husband; the boy's father.

There was one dray horse in the leathers. It was confused and frightened, and was no help because it was unable to get traction and close to foundering as well. Fearful and confused, it whinnied and reared up, which made matters worse.

The boy, also helpless and tearful, stood close to his frantic mother. When he looked north, he spotted the approaching gringos. "Mama! Look! Someone is coming!" He smiled up at her ruefully.

His mother straightened from her desperate task and looked as well. She put her hand to her eyes and smiled. Then her smile became a frown as she gripped her son's shoulder.

"They will help!" the boy shouted.

"Perhaps," his mother said.

The gringos rode up single file through the thick brush, Clyde in the lead. T.J., with a sappy grin, was immediately behind him. Bert and Barney followed a few yards behind.

The draft animal settled momentarily, then continued to paw the ground and whinny.

Clyde and the others stopped and gathered around the scene as their horses reacted, agitated and nervous.

The frightened woman, the boy and the four riders, all looked at each other and the man on the ground in silence. Her eyes betrayed her fear as she pulled her son in close.

Clyde behaved as though he didn't know the trouble the little family was in. "What seems to be the trouble, ma'am?" He pushed his hat back in an insincere gesture.

T.J. maneuvered his horse to a position where he could see what was in the wagon. It consisted of a few paltry personal belongings.

Bert and Barney continued to hang back as they tried to sooth their mounts.

The woman spoke in Spanish. "My husband—he is badly injured. His leg—can you help us?" She pointed to the suffering man under the wheel.

Bert finally rode closer, followed by Barney. Neither wanted trouble, especially Barney, who believed they were being followed. He looked back toward La Bajada, then more closely at the woman. He was struck by her beauty, and stared.

He saw that she had clear, smooth, slightly swarthy skin, green eyes, reddish hair and fine features. She was slight, with a very feminine figure, obvious even under the many layers of cloth she wore.

The other three gringos glanced at each other silently.

Bert scowled at Clyde and jerked his head to indicate they should move on.

Clyde looked at Bert, then the woman. He didn't know what she said, but he knew its meaning. He removed his hat, gestured, and spoke slowly, as though she would understand the English. "Don't know all yore sayin', ma'am, but it looks like a tough job. We'll ride on ahead an' send some help. Team o' horses. Sorry." With that, he settled his hat, touched the brim and clicked his tongue at his horse.

The woman, confused, responded with "What?!"

Bert, relieved at Clyde's decision, said, "Good idee. We'll do that." He pointed at the injured man. "He'll be alright. *All-right.*" He shouted the last two words, as though she would understand, nodded, tipped his hat, then started off.

T.J. smiled disingenuously at the panicked woman. "Y'all wouldn't have some money on ya', would ya'? Might have ta' pay somebody."

She looked up at him, and spoke again in Spanish. "Sir?"

T.J. pointed at the mired wheel and cocked his head. "Dinero. For the help."

The woman held her hands out in total frustration. She pleaded, "I don't understand. We have no money. Please! My husband—!" She gestured toward the incapacitated man.

Clyde reined his horse in and turned back. "Aw' right, boys. 'Nough. Let's git. Gotta' find help fer these folks." He looked at the woman. "How far to help, ma'am?"

"What?!" She cried.

Bert broke his silence. "Goddamnit, Clyde, she don't understand a word! C'mon!"

"Shit!" Clyde exclaimed. "Wish Whitey was here."

T.J. growled, "Goddamnit! They gotta' have somethin' here!"

Bert pulled in close to T.J. and gave him a hard look. "T.J., for once in your life, think 'o someone 'sides yoreself!" He threw out his arm. "These folks ain't got nothin' but trouble! If we was real men, we'd help 'em! Since we ain't, least we can do is ride on an' leave 'em be 'afore some other dumb fuckin' idee gits in yore brain!"

T.J. glared back at Bert and fingered the butt of his pistol. Bert matched his stare until T.J. looked away and whipped his horse's flanks with the reins.

All four gringos rode up and out of the river basin onto the plateau.

Barney came last with two things on his mind. One, the distant rider he saw, and two, the woman at the wagon. He continued to look back.

Bert came alongside T.J. but didn't look at him. "Don't ever threaten me with that iron again, T.J."

T.J. looked at Bert as though injured. "What'er yew goin' on about?! I never—"

Bert swung his head to look at T.J. "Don't mess with me, T.J. Next time, you better jerk it all the way, 'cause mine'll be out an' spittin' lead! You hear?!"

T.J. looked aside in an angry pout as Bert pulled away to ride alone.

Barney rode up to be alongside Bert. "Damn! That was a purty woman!" He tilted his head side to side to emphasize his words.

T.J. overheard. "She was a Mex."

Barney looked back at T.J., then at Bert, a question on his features. "How could that be?"

Bert said, quietly, "Not all Mexicans are dark. She's Spanish."

"Spanish?" Barney asked. His voice gained in pitch.

"Spanish come from Spain, Barney. That's in Europe. They're like us." Bert gestured with his hand, but continued to look ahead as he jogged in the saddle.

"Shit you say," Barney said. He waited, then, "I'm goin' back."

Bert looked at the young man, incredulous. "What?!"

Barney answered, "Decided to help."

Bert and Barney stopped as Bert stared wildly at the red-haired youth.

"How?! Bert shouted. "You ain't got no tools! You'd hafta' use your horse!" He gestured angrily.

Barney, resolute, turned his horse to face north toward the giant stream bed. Unfazed, he said, "I'll git a board 'er somethin'."

Bert turned his body in the saddle to face Barney as his horse rocked his head up and down in protest. "That's plumb loco, Barney!" He paused, then added, "We ain't waitin.'" He held a finger up.

Barney had begun to move away.

After a few seconds, as he continued to face the disappearing youth, Bert shouted, "Better hurry. We'll be down river."

At the site of the mired wagon, the boy looked up to see Barney ride down onto the river plain. Suspicious and frightened, he tugged at his mother's skirt and pointed. She stood up from her futile labors with her injured husband and looked as well.

Barney approached at a slow walk. As he came closer, he manufactured a phony smile and gestured toward the disaster on the ground. He then dismounted and made his way through the thick brush to the edge of the mired wagon. He became falsely serious as he bent down to look more closely at the wheel that was on top of the man's obviously broken leg. His mind was, in reality, on the woman, covered in mud and bits of plant life here and there, who stood next to him.

He straightened and surveyed the area. "We need some brush. A tree—" He pulled the hunting knife that was sheathed at his belt line and made a cutting motion. "Brush—trees!"

The woman, somewhat relieved, nodded in understanding. She awarded him a pained smile.

Barney made his way to a thicket of young willows, then beckoned her to follow. She did, but not before signaling her son to remain with his father. Then, she and Barney trudged farther into the thicket to a medium-sized willow, where Barney began to use his knife on its branches.

It was then that Severino arrived at the north shore of the Rio Salado. He stopped to survey the *arroyo* and decided where to cross. As he roved his eyes along the length of the flat streambed, he noticed motion on the opposite side. Although wary of exposing himself to danger, his instinct was to face it. He goaded his horse, and he and the animal made their way across. The well-trained and experienced horse dodged wet spots expertly on the way.

As Severino crossed the partially wet intermittent river, Barney and the woman cut and gathered willow branches. They became physically close, such that Barney was able to sense the woman's aura and faint, feminine smell. He was unable to concentrate as his passion rose.

Grateful for his return and participation, when he turned to look at her, she smiled up at him. Unable to control himself, he gave in to his desire, dropped the knife, pulled her in close and forced a kiss on her mouth. She tried to struggle free and cry out, but Barney was half again her size and held his hand over her mouth. They lost balance, and fell to the messy ground.

Severino arrived at the scene of the mired wagon, looked around and greeted the boy from the saddle. Then they both heard a scream come from the thicket a few yards away. Severino and the boy looked in that direction, then he glanced at the child, reined his horse around, and raced toward the sound.

When Severino came upon Barney and the woman, they were on the ground. Barney's pants were down halfway to his knees, he had pulled the woman's ripped dress up, and was trying to force her legs apart.

The woman's son arrived a few seconds behind Severino. Alarmed at the site of his mother being attacked, he grabbed a large piece of fallen willow and began to hit Barney's legs. Barney rolled away, spotted the man on horseback and struggled to pull his pants up. The woman gathered herself and scrambled free. His pants almost to his waist, Barney found his pistol, pointed it in Severino's direction, and pulled the trigger.

Severino, winged in his left arm by the shot, lost his balance, started to slip off the saddle, regained his balance, straightened, and went for the gun at his side. Barney took advantage of the delay, grabbed his knife, and with one hand holding his pants up, raced away through the dense reeds to his patiently waiting mount. Severino pointed his firearm toward the escaping man, but lowered the gun and holstered it in favor of reaching for the painful, bleeding wound in his left arm. He dismounted.

Meanwhile, the woman and her son had returned to the stricken wagon. He led his horse as he followed.

When he came up to the woman and the her son, both of whom

looked at him in wonder, he asked, "What happened here?" He grimaced with the pain as blood seeped down his arm and stained his sleeve.

The woman, badly shaken, said, "He attacked me—he came back to help, but—" She shook her head, looked down, then back up at Severino.

Severino nodded at her unconscious husband beneath the wheel. "Who is this?" He held the reins.

She looked at his wound. "You're bleeding!"

Severino shook his head. "I'm alright. What happened to him?" He dropped the horse's reins, and the animal held steady.

The woman ignored his question, bent down to rip some cloth from the hem of her mostly-destroyed dress, then wrapped it around his wound.

He looked at her and nodded. "Thank you. What happened?" He gestured with his chin.

As Severino leaned over to look at the wheel and the man's leg, she said, "The wagon—my husband—"

Severino said, "It's broken."

The boy crowded in close to Severino. "Are you a doctor?"

He looked at the boy. "No. I saw army surgeons care for the wounded." He straightened and looked around. "We need to make a splint." He caressed his bandaged wound.

"Splint?" the boy asked.

Severino looked down at him. "Yes. Something stiff to make his leg straight and not move." He looked around again, then down. "We need to get the wheel off of him."

Under Severino's direction and assistance, the three gathered as much dry foliage as they could find, then placed it under all four wheels of the wagon. Severino then lashed his horse alongside the draft animal still in harness at the front of the wagon. He mounted his horse, then with shouts and gestures, encouraged both animals to move. At the same time, the woman and her son pushed the wagon from the rear. The vehicle lurched and jerked, then became free and moved forward until Severino guided it onto high ground and the main, safe trace that crossed the river plain.

Severino managed to remove two wooden slats from the distressed wagon and return to the injured man, his wife and son with those and rope from his saddlebags. Without a word, he and the woman straighten her husband's leg, arranged the slats on the broken limb and bound them with rope. With the makeshift splint in place, the three of them carried the still unaware man to the wagon bed.

With his right hand over the bloody cloth on his left arm, Severino looked at the woman. "Are you able to drive the wagon?" He winced.

Her eyes betrayed affection as she looked up at him. "Yes." She started to weep, then held back. "The angels sent you. How can we repay you?"

Severino looked toward the south. He ignored her question. "Did you see some gringos—*Tejanos*—who rode this way?" He looked at her. "That boy—"

She became agitated and waved her arms. "Four of them! They would not help, but one—that one—returned!"

"He was one of them?!" He looked toward the south and thought of Tito's description and the men he had seen in the bawdy house.

"Yes!" She nodded emphatically.

He looked at her again. "How long did the others leave?"

"One hour? No more." She shrugged, then shook her head.

"Where did you come from?"

"Bernalillo. We have traveled since last night." She nodded with a smile.

"Where are you going?"

"Santa Fé."

"That is a long way."

She pointed west, down stream. "There are Indians that way. And a church. We will go there."

"Good luck."

She pointed at his injured arm. "Your arm. You need help."

"I will be fine. The bullet passed through." He smiled ruefully.

"God be with you." She tilted her head and smiled sadly as she twisted her hands together.

Severino mounted his horse, then spurred him to a gallop.

The woman and her young son watched as he rode up the slope to the plateau and disappeared over the edge.

Barney found his three trail partners in a clearing in the *bosque* next to the Rio Grande after an hour-long ride. He was greeted with a grunt by T.J., a long, curious look by Bert, and no response from Clyde, who was in the process of spreading his bed roll out on the leaf and twig-strewn river playa.

Bert wandered about as he inspected the area. He looked up into the tall cottonwoods, while T.J. had settled against the base of a tree, and had picked up a fallen twig and begun to whittle.

Barney lead his mount to the shallow stream to be alongside the other horses, dropped the reins, then walked away, anxious to avoid the others and any questions they might pose.

As Clyde settled onto his blanket with a piece of jerky, Barney returned to his horse, opened a saddlebag, and retrieved some paper. He started for the edge of the clearing and into the thick underbrush. "I'm goin' o'er yonder. Gotta' go."

T.J., who had made several cuts into the tiny stick, tested it on his teeth. Without looking up, he said, "Don't fergit to wipe yore Mess-kin." He smirked and let out a single "Hah!"

The others ignored him; especially Barney, who smarted severely from his failed rendezvous. He threaded his way into the thick underbrush until he found a small, hidden open area. There, he prepared himself by unbuckling and lowering his pants and assuming a squat.

Severino had raced to catch up enough to the youth to see him ride into the riverside *bosque*. He slowed, stopped, dismounted and waited on the plateau above the great river plain as he pondered his next move. He hunkered down on his boots, his horse's reins held loosely in one hand. A few minutes after his arrival, he saw movement in the rushes below and stood to look more closely. A moment later he saw a hat, then a swatch of reddish hair, and realized who it was. He took the quirt from the saddle pommel, soothed his horse, then made his way quickly and quietly down the slope to the verdant plain.

Barney, settled into a brief but necessary routine, heard movement in the rushes, but ascribed it to food-searching birds or other small creatures. Other than that, he felt safe. His judgement was verified when he saw a turtle dove flutter up from the reeds to fly to a nearby cottonwood. He thought of the woman and how close he had come to conquer her.

The next time he became aware of rustling was when the sound came from behind. By the time he faintly realized it represented danger, it was too late for him to react. Severino had circled carefully and leaped from the edge of the little clearing to deftly throw the quirt around Barney's throat and pull hard with one knee on the boy's back.

Barney reacted violently, but silently, as his hands flailed against the attack, since the pressure against his throat prevented him from crying out. He thrashed to the very end, then went heavily limp in breathless death. Severino laid him out on his stomach, his trousers still in disarray, then leaned down and ripped his shirt open.

In the clearing along the river literal, T.J. dozed off against the tree where Barney had last seen him. Bert stood and threw what few rocks he could find into the shallow brown water that flowed slowly by. Clyde, having abandoned his bed roll and returned it to his horse's flank, sat on a fallen tree trunk and chewed on a second piece of jerky.

He chewed, then, his mouth not completely clear of the dried meat, asked, "What the hell's keepin' that boy?" He glanced at the place where Barney had disappeared.

T.J. popped awake. "Prob'ly fell in." He snickered.

Clyde, his mouth full again, spoke against the mass of food. He gestured. "Horse's still here."

Bert, short of rocks, turned to look toward the place where he had seen Barney disappear. "Better go look," he said, then walked in that direction.

T. J. closed his eyes again.

Finished with the jerky, Clyde garnered his knife and began to pick his teeth with it.

Thirty seconds passed, then they heard Bert's shouts. "Clyde! T.J.! Over here! Quick!"

The two resting men took a full three seconds to look at each other, then rose to follow the now beaten path through the stand of reeds.

Bert, who stood, bent, next to Barney's body, breathed in gulps as he surveyed the death scene. His eyes were wide and feral.

Clyde came up behind him, stood and stared down. T.J. was a second behind, and did the same. All were speechless; frozen with fear.

Barney was face down in the dirt, his buttocks exposed, his shirt ripped up the middle. Three long, red welts decorated his fair-skinned back.

Bert's voice was a low growl. "We got us a gen-u-wine problem here." He looked away at nothing, then back at Clyde to stare at him, wide-eyed. He breathed hard and fast, his mouth slack. His heart pounded.

T.J.'s voice quavered with fear and loathing. "It's them goddamn Mess-kins up north!" There was a touch of pathetic, fearful weeping to his voice. He paced away in a tight circle, bent over.

"I don't plan to get bumped by no religious greaser!" Clyde exclaimed. His voice was barely above a whisper. He looked around with a glare, then at Bert and T.J. in turn. He lowered his voice to a conspiratorial level. "Listen." He paused as he gulped his fear back. "We gotta' think this out." He looked around again at nothing. "We gotta' start guardin' each other." He looked at T.J. "T.J., you take the first watch." He gestured with a dismissive wave of his hand.

T.J., still bent over with fear and loathing, hardly able to function, pointed at his own chest. He looked up at Clyde with his mouth curled in anguish. "Me?! What's wrong with me just high-tailin' it outa' here an' leavin' you smart fellers to figure it out?! You started this fuckin' mess!" He glared first at Clyde, then Bert, then forced himself to straighten and turned away.

Clyde stepped over Barney's body toward T.J. "You sorry, no-good—!"

Bert wheeled around to face the other two. His voice became a hoarse whisper. "Shut up, the two a' ya'!" He glared at both in turn.

T.J. and Clyde stopped their confrontation and stared at Bert, who continued to glare at them. All three fell silent for several seconds. They were a-sea.

Bert straightened, took a deep breath, exhaled, and continued. His voice and demeanor were commanding. "Stop fightin' twixt the two 'o ya' an' think! Think, goddamnit! Whoever's doin' this wants us to fight. Split us up. We gotta' stick together, least ways 'til we get well down river." He paused as he swallowed hard, looked at the ground and around while breathing deeply again in an attempt to control his fear and anger. He straightened, arched his back and looked at T.J. His fists were clenched at his sides. "Now Clyde's idee is a good 'un. We need to watch out more. An' if you take off by yourself, T.J., they're bound to git yew." He pointed at the deceased youth. "Lookie here."

The three men looked at each other in silence as their eyes danced with fear.

T.J. took a breath and let it out. He spoke in low tones. "Okay. But let's git outa' *here*!" He nearly shouted the last word.

"Just hold on," Bert, his voice shaking, said solemnly. "We gotta' bury the boy."

T.J. turned away, frustrated once again. "Shee-ut."

Clyde thought for a moment, then spoke quietly. "He's right. Look around, but keep us in sight."

T.J. stared at Clyde, then Bert, then jerked his Colt's revolver from its holster, backed away, turned, and began to prowl nervously.

Clyde and Bert grabbed Barney's feet and dragged his body back toward the river-side clearing.

13

After taking out revenge on Barney, Severino returned to his patient horse, took up the reins, patted the animal on his snout, cooed something soothing, and mounted. He looked again down the draw he had selected that ran toward the *bosque*, then turned his mount in the other direction. He rode a quarter mile east, up the slanting piedmont at the base of the Sandia Mountain, then stopped behind a large juniper-cedar. There, he searched the lower horizon under the shade of his hat brim, and saw no activity. He looked north, then south with the same result. He decided to wait, and leaned on the saddle pommel to watch. He felt that his vigil would be rewarded.

After unceremoniously digging a shallow grave and burying the nineteen year-old fatherless Barney in the river clearing, Clyde, Bert and T.J. solemnly rode out of the Rio Grande watershed and up onto the open piedmont. They rode on a sweep of dun grama grass pock-marked with bushy juniper-cedar that rarely exceeded fifteen feet in height. The sloping, undulating plain was dominated by the immense Sandia massive to their left and the wide, flat verdant valley of the Rio Grande on their right as they rode south. With the lengthening shadows of the afternoon, they were individually more acute to the possibility of ambush and loss of life. They kept their own counsel out of mistaken pride, an unfounded sense of manhood, and increasingly, their failure to understand their predicament. All three turned their heads to look about often; especially to the north. They saw no man or animal.

They had eaten sparingly, their picnic at the river having been interrupted. They were thirsty, hungry, tired and anxious in the extreme. They rode abreast.

Clyde said, his voice barely audible, "I could use some hot grub."

"Me, too," T.J. muttered.

Bert looked to his rear, then remarked, "I don' know. I reckon we oughta' skip Alb' kirk, chew some jerky an' keep goin.'"

Clyde turned his entire body in the saddle to spend several seconds scanning the northern horizon. He faced around. "Hell, there's nobody out there." Insecurity invaded the timbre of his voice, and the others detected it.

"T.J. shot Clyde a wild look, but said nothing.

"How'd Barney die? Coyotes?" Bert's question dripped with disdainful sarcasm as he moved his head about. He shot Clyde a nasty glance.

Clyde sneered and fondled his whip. "I'd like to meet up with that vermin. We oughta' lay a trap."

Bert twisted his torso to look hard at Clyde. He shouted, "What kinda' trap, fer Chrissakes?!" He threw out his balled fist.

T.J. shook his head. "An I'm the bait, right?"

Clyde reined his horse to a stop. "No. Listen. It'll work."

Bert and T.J. halted and turned their mounts toward Clyde. All three horses dipped their long necks to feast on the tall dun grass at their feet.

Bert shook his head in disbelief and peered at Clyde from under his eyebrows. "How?" He tilted his head from side to side in annoyance.

Clyde gestured. "Sun's nearly set." He waved his hand vaguely at the sky. "We ain't seen nobody. Most likely means they're behind us, but even if they ain't, we set up a picket line from here down to them trees." He paused, looked around, then continued, "One of us stays up here. One in the middle. One takes the point. There, where the land drops off. We git the horses outa' sight, git low ourselves. We stay in sight 'o one another. Watch fer our man. When we git 'im in our sights—"

Bert looked away, unconvinced. He looked at Clyde again. "Man or men, Clyde?!" His mouth was firm.

T.J. tilted his head at Clyde, then Bert. "Hey! It might work!"

Bert turned back. "It's gettin' dark. An' what if there's more than one of 'em, damn it?!"

Clyde, agitated, snarled, "We pick 'em off, goddamnit!" He breathed hard, calmed, looked down, then up. "We got an hour 'o light. "They'll think we've gone on."

Bert acquiesced silently, then nodded without enthusiasm.

T.J., animated, said, "I like it! Least ways, we do somethin'!" He awarded his partners a broad grin.

Severino had watched the three gringos ride up out of the river basin onto the piedmont, then observed them as they headed south. He remained in hiding as they moved along the mostly flat, but occasionally rolling land without attempting to hide. At times they disappeared down into arroyos that delivered rain and snow melt to the river plain, then re-appeared on the other side. He moved from juniper to juniper, careful to avoid discovery. As dusk approached, he saw them stop and appear to argue among themselves.

On foot, Clyde took the reins of all three horses and lead them down off the piedmont and into the river valley among trees and undergrowth where they were hidden from view. As he returned, Bert and T.J. moved down into a shallow *arroyo,* then worked their way up to establish their positions.

Severino watched their progress, then tethered his horse to a tree branch and made an educated guess. He looked around and spotted a large jagged stone. He crept to it as he watched them, picked it up, then tested its heft from a prone position. He spotted a Spanish Sword plant, crept to it, and cut off one of the long, green spears. Back at his horse, he stripped the spear to its core to find long, string-like tendrils. These, he wound into a thin, strong rope substitute. One end he wrapped around the stone, then tested its heft by dangling it toward the ground. He sipped water from his canteen, removed his carbine from its scabbard, then hid behind the ball-shaped tree. He watched and waited as the sun crested the western horizon, and shadows became less distinct. He looked at the mountain behind him. Reddish-orange sunlight continued to brighten its magnificent rocky face as it crawled slowly up to the crest.

He waited another ten minutes as the sky darkened, then dropped to the ground and began to crawl carefully, a few feet at a time, toward the point where he last saw his closest quarry, T.J. He moved slowly and cautiously between plants and rocks with the carbine and the sling held in front of him, military fashion.

T.J. lay on his stomach, his legs spread wide, in a shallow depression toward the beginning of the *arroyo* in a place only deep enough to hide his form. His hat was off and beside him. In both hands, held nervously, was his pistol, pointed generally north. He felt very alone, and looked every few seconds toward Bert, in the center, who was fading from view with the diminishing light.

Bert had assumed the same stance as T.J., several yards along, west, and in a deeper part of the dry bed. Hatless as well, his gun at the ready, he looked often at his partners who waited in the waning gray light.

Clyde occupied the farthest point along the dry runoff bed, west. He was also bare-headed, prone and watched carefully, his pistol gripped tightly.

Severino, meanwhile, continued to crawl slowly, carefully and without a sound toward T.J.'s position. He raised his bare head a second at a time every few feet to check on the man closest to him, then at the one in the middle. Twice, he winced and soothed his wounded, tortured arm by rubbing it.

He stopped moving when he was within a few feet of the eastern-most man. When he figured the light had faded as much as he could allow, he found a small stone and threw it past T.J. such that it landed with a thud beyond the man, on his south side.

T.J. reacted to the sound by turning his body to his right, in the direction of the sound and looked that way. Like a feral cat, he scanned the ground in front him, but made no move other than his head and arms.

Severino took the opportunity to move closer; a mere few feet distant. T.J. did not see or hear him in the faint light.

Severino raised to his knees, swung the stone on the rope over his head, and let fly. The stone struck T.J. on the back of his head, and it dropped to the ground as though dead weight, without utterance. He was on his stomach, his face against the dirt. Severino crawled to him, laid on top of him, then used his quirt to strangle, then whip him after ripping his shirt.

Severino's action was unseen, but Bert, several yards to the west, thought he heard something unidentifiable. He waited, listened, then settled. After a few seconds of reflection, he looked in T.J.'s direction, and was confused by what little he could see in the fading light. He called out in a hoarse whisper, "T.J.!" He waited two seconds, then, "T.J.!" He looked toward Clyde, then back toward T.J.'s position, but detected no movement. He decided to move closer to T.J. so he could hear him. He crouched along the narrow defile, then called out two more times with no result. When he finally arrived, and realized the truth, he whispered, "Jesus fucking Christ!"

In a half-crouch, he made his way back past his assigned lookout point to where Clyde remained on watch. He slid along the dirt next to Clyde. He panted loudly.

"What—?!" Clyde cried out.

"He's dead!" His voice was above a whisper. He pointed. "He's dead! T.J.'s dead!"

Clyde looked past Bert in the semi-dark. "Fuck!"

"We been spooked, Clyde! This ain't workin'!" He was frantic.

"We gotta' git' Now!"

"He's been whipped, Clyde!"

Clyde rose up on all fours, uncaring that the muzzle of his revolver was in the dirt. "Leave 'im! Git his saddlebags! Fuck everything else!"

Severino lay on his stomach a few yards away from T.J.'s body in the direction of where his patient steed waited. He was unable to make out the words of the two men to the west along the *arroyo*, but he heard them, and watched as their vague figures scrambled away in the near dark.

Clyde and Bert, their minds and bodies totally shaken, stumbled along the remainder of the crevice and into the thick cottonwood-dominated planar literal of the Rio Grande in near total darkness. There, they found and removed the saddlebags from T.J.'s horse, then threaded their way deeper into the *bosque*, as they lead their mounts on foot. They spent the night, shivering in the dark, their pistols in their hands, dozing off, then awakening to minor noises in fear for their lives. They had lost their appetites and ate nothing, but sipped water from their canteens.

Neither spoke a word until dawn.

14

Severino cold-camped where he had left his horse. Aside from a short, disturbing dream, he slept well. He feasted on jerky wrapped in a tortilla and drank canteen water before he fell asleep, and at dawn when he awakened. After taking care of essential bodily needs, he offered his grateful horse water in his hand from his canteen, then allowed the animal time to graze on the foot-high grama grass that shared the landscape with the junipers and sage before he saddled him.

He lead the horse on foot along the same *arroyo* where the three gringos had hidden, and where the body of one of them remained. He picked up the pistol and removed the gun belt from the man's body and stowed both in a saddlebag.

He had lost track of the two remaining quarry, but guessed that they would seek food and shelter in Albuquerque. After clearing the *arroyo* on foot, he made his way through the cottonwood forest to the trail that cut through it, then mounted his horse and set out south at a walk.

At first light, Clyde and Bert lead their still-saddled horses on foot through the dense, treed river plane until they found the north-south Santa Fé-Chihuahua Trail that cut through it. They spent almost half the time looking back and scanning the terrain in all directions, completely unsure of who or what to expect. They spoke little, since, in the reality of their plight, both knew they had nothing to offer the other. In their minds, one thing was certain: they must leave the territory, and soon.

They both felt more at ease as they passed the odd house, corral, farm field or orchard and saw people who either glanced their way for a moment or ignored them. As they rode slowly into the northern outskirts of Albuquerque, although they continued to watch their rear, they began to feel better. Hunger and fatigue was the least of their worries. They finally looked at each other and both managed a silent, wan smile and a nod. They were unaware that their pursuer was no more than a mile behind them.

The *cantina* the gringos entered after a look and a nod of understanding, was close to the center of the predominantly adobe village, and along the trail that divided it. It featured a wood-floored portal and a flat, dirt-covered roof that jutted out into the street. A crude sign pegged to the bare adobe wall advertised its purpose.

The two desperate gringos dismounted, lead their horses to the hitching rail and looped the reins. They both stood for a moment and searched the area; especially along the trace they had taken from the north.

Bert approached Clyde as they moved to the porch. He pulled the other man aside and spoke in a low tone. "Ah reckon we should move amongst fellow travelers the remainder of the way."

"Like with a caravan?" Clyde looked at Bert with his head lowered, his face serious. His natural tendency toward arrogance had disappeared

"Exactly."

Clyde nodded. "I think you have somethin.'"

Bert nodded in affirmation, then looked around again.

They both entered.

The room was large, with a low, open-beamed ceiling and a raw wooden floor, new for the territory, where most were of packed, blooded earth. It was somber, although offset somewhat by strategically placed burning oil lamps that hung from the ceiling. Two modern windows that graced either side of the entrance, looked out onto the dirt street with its increasing horse and draft animal-dominated traffic. In the open area, heavy round tables shared the space with an occasional rectilinear style. Most of the seating was of low, pine or hard wood chairs, with some benches present. A long bar that reached nearly from wall-to-wall occupied the rear of the place. Behind it were two mirrors of poor glass that shared the wall with crude shelves of a limited variety of spirits. In the corner opposite the opening in the bar, stood a silent upright piano.

Given that it was morning, there were few patrons, and only a few of them imbibed an alcoholic beverage, while most were engaged in partaking of their morning repast. There were no women. The room reeked of food odors that mingled with those of tobacco smoke and the faint scent of kerosene that stoked the lamps.

Three men bothered to look toward the door when the two remaining trail partners entered. They quickly lost interest and returned to their fare.

The two men walked slowly toward a round table in the rear of the room, close to the piano and the bar. They carried six loaded saddlebags; three each. As they moved, they overheard brief conversation in their native tongue, English. They also noticed the aroma of cooked food. When they reached the table, they set the bags against the wall, then took time to grin at each other with a brief nod of fatigued relief.

Bert looked around, then at Clyde. "I'll go check on some grub."

Clyde nodded approval. "I'll watch our goods." He sat, careful to position his chair to face the door. He caressed his revolver, put his hands on the table, folded them, then took time to look around the room at the other patrons. He didn't allow his eyes to meet with any others for more than an instant.

Bert went to the bar and spoke to the tender, who nodded and went into the back room.

After eating ravenously, and although weary from lack of sleep, both Clyde and Bert had eased into a more comfortable mind-set, and felt energized. More people had arrived, which included two women, some in work attire, some in traveling clothes, there for their initial meal of the day. They saw no military uniforms, and few firearms. They heard more English spoken, which served to relieve them more. After ordering shots of an alcoholic beverage, they were joined by two locals with whom they were able to communicate, and who possessed a deck of cards. The noise level rose, and was soon accompanied by poorly rendered music from the piano by an incidental volunteer. The old man set an empty tumbler on top of the instrument in hopes of spare change for his efforts.

Their plates, utensils, saucers and cups, with evidence of food and drink, still lay on the table where Clyde and Bert sat, along with empty shot glasses at their elbows.

An hour and a half after the apparent salvation of the frightened, desperate gringo pair, the relative peace of the *cantina* was interrupted by a sudden racket. All in the large room, including the bartender and servers, looked in the direction of the noise to see a man standing in the center of the room. He yielded a strange, small wooden device, and swung it several times every few seconds to create a ratcheting sound. Several patrons shouted at him. Others grumbled at each other or grinned in reaction as they shook their heads.

The bartender came around the end of the bar, stopped and shouted for the man to cease and to remove himself. But he was hesitant when he noticed the holstered pistol at the man's waist and the bloody bandage on his upper left arm. Further, the man behaved as though he heard nothing, and looked in one direction only—straight ahead.

Both Clyde and Bert, with their hands occupied with playing cards, looked in Severino's direction, agape. They looked at each other, alarm writ large on their features.

Bert lowered his card hand slowly to the table, pushed back, rose and with a quick brush against the handle of his pistol, turned and took several steps toward Severino.

The room began to clear and chairs fell to the floor with loud thuds as some of the patrons realized that both standing men were armed and appeared to be headed for a confrontation. Some left for the street.

The bartender, fearful of an encounter, pleaded, "I told you to stop, damn it!" His voice had lost some of its bravado.

Again, Severino ignored the request. He stopped momentarily when he saw Bert rise, but continued to swing the *matraca* as Bert walked slowly toward him.

Bert stopped ten feet away from Severino as the noise ceased. "Where'd you find that?!"

Severino put on a face of wide-eyed innocence and shrugged.

Without removing his eyes from Bert's, he gestured toward the outside. "Out there."

"Where? On the ground?!"

"On the ground? No. On a horse." His voice betrayed no fear; more that of amused insolence.

This remark generated scattered nervous laughter among some of those who remained, most of whom stood back and away from the possible line of fire. Neither Bert nor Severino shared their levity. Clyde, meanwhile, was poised on the edge of his chair, his right hand on the handle of his pistol. He was again in shock, and unable to think clearly.

Bert broke the tense silence by chuckling nervously under his breath. He awarded Severino a tolerant grin. He then sobered as his ire escalated. He took a deep breath. "That's not yours," he growled.

Severino raised the *matraca* and peered at it comically. "It think it belongs to my friend." He lowered the noise-maker and stared at Bert with fierce eyes.

"You think—!"

Severino interrupted, "Yes. I know it." He stared hard at Bert, as he watched every move the man made.

Again laughter filled the room, louder this time.

Bert was losing patience, and felt foolish. He breathed hard with his anger. "If you found it on a horse outside, it belongs to me!"

Clyde watched from the table as the two men who had been playing cards with him and Bert, slowly and quietly removed themselves and crept away in a large, split arc around the two armed men who faced each other.

Severino, his eyes feral, said, "Then you must take it from me!"

Bert flinched, and with that, Severino had Chet's .44 out and angled up, pointed at Bert's head. He pulled the hammer back slowly, which made metallic steel-on-steel clicks loud enough to be heard around the now deathly silent room. All but two men, including the bartender, quickly moved or ducked for cover.

Bert froze, his gun still holstered, as his hand hovered over it. He pursed his lips with his tension as his pulse and breath rate rose..

Clyde rose, and his chair fell backward to the floor with a bang. He did not go for his gun; he was too close to the line of fire.

Severino, unaffected by Clyde's action, did not flinch or look in his direction. Rather, he kept his eyes fixed on Bert.

Bert turned his head, shot Clyde a glance, then Severino from the corner of his eye. He forced a smile, lowered his eyes, and swiveled as though to walk away.

Severino pointed his pistol at the ceiling, then at the floor. It was still cocked. He watched Bert carefully as he began to holster the firearm.

Then Bert changed direction, swung about suddenly, and jerked his pistol from its holster at the same time. In a trice, the gun was up and pointed at Severino. "You shit!"

Severino, with his pistol still in his hand, arced it up and fired before Bert could get off a shot. Bert received a clean shot to the head, and although instantly dead, his body remained upright for two seconds before he crumpled backwards to the floor. Severino swung his pistol to point it at Clyde.

Clyde, thunderstruck, was frozen into inaction, and could do no more than stare at the dead body of his long-time trail partner lying on the floor. He looked at Severino, removed his hand from his holster and jerked a quick "no" with his head.

Severino pointed his gun around the nearly empty room as a warning, then at Clyde as he backed out of the *cantina*. The *matraca* was still in his other hand.

He did not run, but rather walked rapidly through the small, but scattering on-lookers who had gathered around the door, to his horse, which he had stationed around the corner of the building. He mounted, looped the *matraca* string around the pommel next to his quirt, then pulled the carbine from the right-side scabbard and spurred the horse forward.

Clyde, dazed, confused and uncertain, stumbled out of the *cantina*, his pistol in his hand, four stuffed saddlebags in the other, with two draped over his shoulders. The crowd scattered for him as he looked about frantically for the man who had gunned his partner down.

Two men pointed in the direction of Severino's escape, but he was too distracted to notice.

He went to his horse, still tethered to the rail immediately in front of the porch, and threw the bags over the animal's back. He did not mount, rather he stood and looked around as he tried to figure out where the assailant had gone. He held his pistol at a defensive crouch. He wiped his mouth in blind frustration as he tried to gather his wits. He lurched aimlessly into the dusty street as a growing crowd watched in fascination.

Women and children arrived, along with a cacophony of speculation in the undulating herd. People laughed, shouted, pointed and aided each others false information with nonsensical chatter.

Severino appeared from around the corner of the building. He was up in the saddle, with the reins looped around the pommel. His carbine was raised to his shoulder in a military attack posture, pointed at the frantic gringo. He controlled his horse with his boots.

Clyde, when he realized the scattering people were looking behind him, swung around to see Severino. Severino raised the long gun higher, and Clyde flung his pistol away to land several feet distant in the dirt. With the carbine still aimed at Clyde, Severino urged his horse forward at a walk.

Clyde hesitated, dashed for his horse and grabbed his whip from the pommel, then raced back into the open street, now a large circle formed by the anticipating, salivating crowd. Severino slid the carbine into its scabbard. Ever defiant, Clyde stood, his feet set wide apart, and glowered at Severino in the saddle. He felt that somehow, the presence of the crowd would avail him an advantage.

Severino took his quirt in hand, the reins in the other, and spurred his mount to race past Clyde. He swiped at the gringo with the quirt, but missed. Clyde turned and waited for Severino to turn and come back. As he did, his quirt outstretched, Clyde managed to wrap his whip around Severino and pull him from the saddle. His horse traveled several yards, then slowed and stopped as his master hit the ground and rolled away, quirt still in hand. Clyde prepared his whip, then lashed out at the man on the ground.

The tip of the whip ripped through Severino's shirt and bloodied his chest. His wounded arm began to bleed again as the makeshift bandage slipped away. As Clyde pulled the whip in to ready it for the next strike, Severino rose to one knee, drew his revolver and leveled it at Clyde. For a few seconds, both men stared at each other as the people who surrounded them went quiet. Then Severino lobbed a shot at Clyde's feet where a puff of dirt rose and struck his boots. Clyde dropped the whip and stepped back, his mouth slack, eyes wide in defeat.

Severino stood, but kept his pistol on Clyde, who now stood still, out in the open space that had cleared for him. He surveyed the puzzled, anxious crowd, then waved his gun at two nearby men. He reached into a saddlebag on his horse that had wandered back, and retrieved a length of raw hide.

He spoke to the men he had selected in Spanish. "You! Help me bind his hands!"

They hesitated and glanced at each other, but with lethal force in the demanding man's hand, moved toward Clyde, who looked around, fearful fire in his eyes. As Severino watched, the two men bound Clyde's hands in front, then to his belt.

Severino commanded, "Help me get him on his horse!"

Clyde, almost docile with his fate, and with assistance, was placed in his saddle. Severino picked up Clyde's whip and gun and mounted his horse.

A commotion arose from the direction of the town center, then the crowd split for two men who marched into the scene. They were the sheriff and his deputy. They were dressed in a semblance of uniforms, both with wide-brimmed hats. The sheriff wore a sidearm, while the deputy brandished a long gun.

The sheriff stopped, looked around, then at the two men on horseback. He spoke in Spanish. "What's going on here?!"

Many voices chimed in with various accounts of the situation. They crowded in, pointed, shouted; some used words such as "murderer," "brigand," "thief," and the like.

"Quiet! Silence!" The sheriff shouted. He waved his arms, then looked up at Clyde, then Severino. "Who are you?! What's this about?!"

The crowd quieted as Severino moved his horse closer to the sheriff. He held the reins to Clyde's horse and continued to aim his carbine at the sequestered man. He pointed and spoke in Spanish. "This man and the dead man inside. They are criminals. They attacked my village. Six of them. They killed my brother and an old man. They shamed a young girl. They took my brother's wife and shamed her. She is also dead. I am here to take this man back with me. He will face our justice."

The crowd became vociferous again with wild gestures and unintelligible shouted remarks.

The sheriff held up his hand and shouted, "Silence! Silence!" He looked up at Severino. "How do I know this?! Who are you?!"

"My name is Severino Torres. Of San Blas. I swear by the holy mother and the name of my parents that what I say is true." He made the sign of the cross. "I am here to take this man. Do not stop me, or by my oath, I will kill him here and now for what he and his band have done!" He reasserted his aim at Clyde. "I do not care for my life. This I swear!"

The people who watched and listened save for a murmur here and there, became dead silent as the sheriff and Severino studied each other's faces. Clyde understood little of what was said, but lowered his head to his chest in profound understanding of his fate.

The sheriff looked around. Many in the crowd nodded assent. He looked up at Severino and spoke in a low voice. "I believe you. Go now. If you come back, I will arrest you."

Severino nodded somberly, lowered the carbine and stowed it in the scabbard. He then took up the reins from Clyde's horse and the two mounted animals moved slowly away. Some in the crowd, principally young boys, followed for a short distance, then fell away.

15

In the early morning, shortly after dawn, a young boy carried a wooden bucket to the village well. He looked east, toward the crest of the Sangre de Cristo mountains with the sun barely above it. He whistled a simple tune. Then he stopped his private music, stared, set the bucket down, then started a slow walk in the direction of *Calvario*. After a moment, eyes wide, he turned and ran. "Mama! Papa!"

In a few minutes, townspeople emerged from their houses into the frigid mountain air. They gathered, silent, singly and in small groups, in awe, to move slowly toward the sacred hill.

Their faces expressed utter amazement and wonder at what they saw. Only murmurs were uttered.

As they gathered on the hill, they formed a rough circle to stand and stare at one of the criminal crosses.

Clyde, his nearly naked, pale body with only a piece of cloth over his loins, had been bound with horsehair to the cross. Although unconscious, he shivered violently. His mouth was open and drooling. Save for his face, which exhibited a bruise around his mouth and a bloody nose, his body bore no marks or bruises.

His unburdened horse was tethered to the other cross reserved for a faux criminal. His clothes lay on his nearby saddle, which was on the ground. His pistol belt hung from the pommel. The saddlebags were missing. On the ground at the feet of Clyde's cross was his whip. At the base of the re-erected center cross, carefully folded, was Nicanora's *reboso*. On top of that was the *matraca*. Propped against the cross was Santo's carbine in its scabbard.

Nicanora joined the crowd when she learned of the event taking place on the sacred hill. She moved through the gathering toward the cross where Clyde hung, then saw her *reboso*. Her somber expression turned to joyful tears as she looked across the ravine at Severino's house. Then she began a slow walk in that direction.

Severino rode his horse at a walk along a Santa Fé side street. His carbine was in its scabbard, his bedroll behind his saddle. Along with his saddlebags were those taken from the gringos, which bulged with stolen loot. Chet's pistol was not in evidence, hidden in a saddlebag, but Severino's Indian knife was on his belt, and the quirt hung from the pommel.

He halted near the office of the sheriff and looked about. Soon, he spotted a young man who walked by. "Hey!"

The young man stopped and looked up. He spoke in Spanish. "I?"

Severino turned in the saddle to retrieve the heavy saddlebags, then looked down. "Yes. A moment, please." He held the bags out. "Would you give these to the sheriff?"

The youth reached for the bags. "Of course, but why?"

"Tell him they are from the robbery. Tell him to look for Tito. Will you?"

"Yes, but who are you?"

Severino smiled and saluted with two fingers to the brim of his hat. "Many thanks." With that, he clicked his horse forward and headed for the edge of town and the terminus of the Santa Fé Trail.

Pronouncing Gazetteer

Abuelo: ah-BWELL-oh. Grandfather.

Aguardiente: ah-wahr-DYENT-thay. One version is literally, "to guard the teeth." The formal version is the rough translation, "fire water." A potent alcoholic beverage from Mexico whose source was "whatever is available," which often included fermented cactus juice.

Arroyo: ah-ROY-oh. Creek; gulch; minor tributary. In New Mexico, more often dry, but potentially dangerous with thunderstorm conditions. The double "r" is trilled such that it sounds much like a soft English "d."

Banco: BAHN-coh. Bench, in this context. In another, a place where money is kept.

Bosque: BOSS-kay. A literal forest, generally applied to the cottonwood groves that line the Rio Grande in the "middle river" area (Bernalillo, Albuquerque and points south).

Bueno: BWEN-oh. Good. Okay.

Cantina: cahn-TEEN-ah. Canteen; generally a place of business where libations are served, more often than not accompanied by viands.

Dueña: DWEN-yah. Although defined differently in Spain, in this context an older, generally married female escort for young, unmarried girls when in public. Still practiced in New Mexico villages as late as the mid-twentieth century.

Doña: DOHN-yah. Lady, as in, for example, "her ladyship."

Floresta: flo-REST-ah. Forest.

Grama grass: GRAH-mah. Ubiquitous in the far Mid- and upper Midwest and Southwest, this dun-colored grass, unlike green grass, is roughly 90% nutrient and 10% water, versus the reverse in the green plant. As such, it is an excellent food enjoyed by bison, European cattle and western antelope alike. From western Kansas, Oklahoma and Texas, Colorado, New Mexico and north to Montana and Wyoming, it is prized. It requires no "salt" or other "licks," as it is a complete food. The seed is available commercially.

La Bajada: lah bah-HAH-thah. The Descent. The steep road between the Middle Rio Grande Valley and the plateau region west and south of the Sangre de Cristo mountains. Treacherous until modern times.

Latias: Also latillas. lah-TEE-yahss. Straight, thin stripped cedar employed as a finished ceiling between vigas (see below), often arranged in an offset herringbone pattern.

Morada: more-ATH-ah. In classical Spanish, a home or resting place. In this context, more as a place of heaven, the final resting place. The name used for the secret *Penitente* gathering place.

Pantalones: pahn-tah-LONE-ess. Pants.

Ponchos: POHN-choss. A unitary cape- or blanket-like apparel, used for protection against the elements, similar to a cape, that drapes over the entire body with a hole provided centered for the head.

Piñon: peen-YOHN. Although the "on" ending indicates large size, this evergreen pine tree, so abundant throughout New Mexico's mountainous regions, is a lesser size pine, especially when compared to the magnificent ponderosa pine. The tree gives a periodic shower of small, hard-shelled nuts, highly prized throughout New Mexico and the southwest by squirrels, humans and the occasional dog, and invites hordes of fanatics to search the ground for them when in season. Perhaps the source of the name.

Portal: por-TAHL. Porch.

Pueblo: PWEB-loh. In this context, "town." Also "people," or "peoples."

Rio Salado: Sah-LAH-thoh. Saline; salty.

Sangre. SAHNG-gray. Blood. The "g" takes a hard pronunciation.

Santo Domingo: sahn-toh doh-MING-goh. Holy Sunday.

Tejano: tay-HAHN-oh. Texan.

Tienda: tthee-YEN-dah. Store. The leading "t" is softened with a trailing "th" sound.

Torres: TOR-ess. Surname meaning Towers. The "r" is pronounced like a soft English "d" with a hint of "r" leading it.

Tules: TTHOO-less. Reeds.*

Viga: VEE-gah. Ceiling beam.

Yeso: YESS-oh. A simple gypsum-based white paint. Used for many years in the southwestern U.S. before the arrival of commercial paints. Adheres well to mud-plastered adobe walls.

*Doña Tules (Lady Reeds; purportedly because she was thin) was a real figure in the Territory of New Mexico during the period of this story; in some minds, infamous. Although there is solid evidence of her running a gambling den centered around her favorite game, monte, it is not clear that she also ran a bordello, or that if so, her place contained two stories. For those history purest who take umbrage at this passage, I beg forbearance and forgiveness for my trespass. The story simply works better as written.

—The author.